SLIM SIRINGO
'DERECHOS'
PERSISTENT WIND
BOOK #7

DAVID W. BAILEY

For information contact: info@outlawspublishing.com
Cover design by Outlaws Publishing LLC
Published by Outlaws Publishing LLC
August 2024
10987654321

Chapter One

Those Swinging Doors

The United States government was in a weakened state during the 1860s. It was well known that if Lincoln won the election for president, he would not take office until March 4 of 1861. It was also known he was not interested in dealing with the problem of secession before he took office. The outgoing President, James Buchanan, had stated that by the Constitution, secession was illegal. He, also shared his opinion by saying that it was illegal for the United States government to try and prevent southern states from seceding from the union. It seemed he was showing signs of fear to tackle that situation as it was too close to him leaving the office of the president of the United States, so he declined, and would not accept his party's nomination for president. There were members of Congress who tried to work out compromises to satisfy the southerners, but those compromises did not succeed. President Buchanan all but left the office of president, and it showed in his behavior.

Early that morning in the diner of Comanche, Oklahoma, Karl Stokes and Paul Stroud was having their breakfast. Both men seemed to be nervous to the point that they, at times, stopped to look around themselves.

Karl looked across the table at Paul saying, "Wade isn't goin' to like what we have to tell him, you know that don't ya?"

Paul swallowed a sip of coffee, then replied, "I know."

Cutting his ham steak, Larry said, "He's goin' to be madder than a wet hen."

"I know that too."

"Well, what're we goin' to do?" Taking a bite of his ham steak, "We're in deep trouble."

"I'm thinkin', Paul." Then, in quieter tones, "Don't bother me while I think."

In whispered tones, "You know as well as I do those miners never gave us a chance to talk to them. It ain't our fault we had to kill one, and then run the other out of the country, is it? Well, is it?" Looking suspiciously around him.

"No, it ain't, but then again, Wade may not see it that way."

"Yeah. That bothers me some, too. I wonder, could we forge their names on that transfer of title deed? No one would know the difference would they?"

"I don't know, Paul. Maybe neither could read, nor write. But, that would be a dead give-away, and Wade would be in a lot of trouble."

"Wade? In trouble? That'll be the day. We're the ones who are in trouble here because we didn't get their signatures on the transfer deed that transferred the mine to Wade."

"I know that's true."

Wade was in his office at the rear of the Lucky Deuce saloon, sitting at his desk doing some paperwork. Every now and then, he would look towards his office door. He was waiting to hear from Paul Stroud, and Karl Stokes about last night. They were to bring him the transfer deed that bore the signatures of both Amos Stegner and Seth Brubaker that transferred their silver mine over to him. He tried to think of something else while he waited. However, he became impatient, so, to kill the time, he left his office, and entered the main floor of the Lucky Deuce saloon. He tried to look nonchalant, and casual with not a worry in the world as he walked around the main room of the saloon. He not only grew impatient, he became a little out of sorts at not hearing from them yet this morning. He walked over to the table where a couple of his hired guns was sitting. As he walked up, the two men looked up to see Wade.

One man said, "Mornin', Wade."

Wade answered, "Mornin', Keith. Emmette. How are you fellas this mornin'?"

Emmette replied, "Fine as frog's hair, thank you."

As he pulled a cheroot from his coat pocket, Wade asked, "Did either of you two go on that night visit last night to the Silver Shovel silver mine with Paul Stroud, and Karl Stokes? They were supposed to have an important document signed for me and they were to bring it back to me so's I can have it recorded."

As Wade lit his cheroot, Keith replied, "We both was there, but as far as we know there was no signing of any document. Was there, Emmette?"

"Not that I remember. All I know is one miner was shot and killed, and the other one was run out a the country."

Wade became angry, but held his tongue for a few seconds even though his face showed his wrath.

In controlled anger, Wade, then asked, "Then, how do you know this other miner was run out of the country?"

Keith replied, "We never did see hide nor hair of him, so we figured he was so down right scared, he left the country."

Wade said, "I see." His mood lightened a little, then he asked, "You two have breakfast yet?"

Keith held up his whiskey glass saying, "Havin' that now, Wade."

"Ah, a liquid breakfast. The same for you, Emmette?"

Emmette raised his glass of whiskey and smiled.

Flynn McDonagh, Seamus O'Neil, and Clancy Burrows mounted their horses and reined them away from Deeb's Livery in Waco, Texas. They nosed their horses out of town towards the pecan grove where Timothy McFadden, and Kevin Taylor are waiting with the wagon of weapons. And, of course there was their friends, Timothy McFadden, and Kevin Taylor. It has been quite some time since they had the chance to get together and talk amongst themselves. It would be such a joy to do that without the threat of any trouble, or having to keep looking over their shoulders. Clancy was quite captivated with these two Irishmen, Timoth McFadden, and Kevin Taylor. He was very much impressed with their attention to detail, and the length they would take to complete their mission. They were, as Flynn and Seamus have been, ever aware of what could happen next, and the way to avoid it, if possible. The only thing he could say about the friends he has recently attained is they are like minded, and loyal to their country, as they should be.

But, unbeknownst to the three men, one of Brass Tacks men had just left the Etsy barn checking wagons and their loads when he saw them ride down main street. The man quickly mounted his horse, and hurriedly went to the Dancing Bear saloon to let Brass Tacks know what he had seen. When the man entered the Dancing Bear saloon, he found Lane with Lilah Silko sitting on his lap, giggling, and them carrying on like school children.

It took a few seconds for the man to say anything, but he knew he had to.

The man, then said, "Lane, I saw 'em." No reaction "I saw 'em, Lane. They was ridin' down main street plain as day."

Lane casually asked, "You saw who, Rex?"

Rex Tibbs replied, "Them Irishmen you're after. Ridin' plain as day down main street."

Lane hurried to his feet, dumping Lilah as he did to the floor to land on her butt.

She shrieked when her butt hit the floor. Giving Lane a look of contempt, she blew a tuft of hair from her face.

Ignoring Lilah, Lane asked, "How long ago."

Rex answered, "No more 'n two minutes ago. I got here as soon as I could."

Lane questioned, "Which way was they headed?"

Rex replied, "You know that pecan grove we passed coming into town?"

Lane replied, "Yeah. So?"

Rex, then said, "They went that way."

Lane scoffed, then said, "You still don't know your east from west, eh, Rex?"

"Maybe I don't, Lane, but I know which way they was goin'."

As Lilah got to her feet, Lane hollered, "Get to your horses!"

As Lane and his men hurried from the saloon, Lilah stomped her feet as she yelled out, "Lane!?"

Mateo looked on in surprise at the goings on, saying, "Ay, caramba!"

Herschel came in from another room as Lilah screamed after Lane.

Herschel turned to Mateo asking, "What did you say to them, Mateo?"

Mateo replied, "Who? Me? I said nothing, Senior." He done the sign of the cross saying, "I swear I said nothing, I think. Ay, chihuahua!"

Herschel asked Lilah, "What happened?"

Still a little perturbed, she answered, "I don't know." sniffling, "Somebody came in sayin' somethin' 'bout seein' some Irishmen," sniffling "ridin' down main street, and off they went for whatever reason." sniffling "Like they've never seen Irishmen before."

Herschel replied, "Hmm, that does sound odd, don't it?" As he was picking up the beer, and whiskey glasses where Lane was sitting, he turned to Mateo saying, "Such a mess. Go grab a soapy water bucket and a mop and mop this area. It's all sticky. Boots sticks to the floor."

Mateo replied, "Si, Senior."

As he went through the door to the storeroom, Mateo was babbling to himself. The only words that were intelligible was, "Ay, chihuahua!", then, the door closed behind him.

A few miles southwest from the small town of Rush Springs, Oklahoma, rode Walt Gratton, Will Ferguson, and Fletcher Sullivan. They were in search of men they knew who could quite possibly be of some help to Slim Siringo and his family as well as those in the town of Comanche, Oklahoma by getting rid of, and taking down Devlin Wade. The scourge of Stephens County.

Fletcher asked, "Are you sure that Creel will be in Rush Springs, Walt?"

Walt replied, "Rush Springs doesn't have a telegraph, Fletch. I had to contact someone who had an idea where Creel could be, and Rush Springs was brought up, as well as a couple other places, but since Rush Springs was the closest. That's where we're goin'. Rush Springs."

Will, then said, "Well, if he ain't there, it has been a long ride for nothin'."

Fletcher, then asked, "Is Jonas Eberly still ridin' with Creel? He and I rode together for a while. That was before I started ridin' with you.""

Walt shrugged his shoulders, then replied, "I don't know."

Will asked, "What about that fella, oh, what's his name? Oh, I remember. Jon Nagle. He was the cat's meow. So friendly with the ladies."

Walt replied, "I don't know that either, but I do remember Thadeus Doucet from New Orleans. Man, he could talk his mother out of her gold teeth. I wonder if he's ridin' with Creel?"

Will, then asked, "Just in case Creel and those men that was mentioned doesn't happen to be in Rush Springs, do you have another plan?"'

Walt replied, "I do. I have more information considering the location of Shane Garraty, Jack Hardee, and Rafe Peterson. But they are farther away than Rush Springs. They're in Texas."

When they entered Rush Springs, the street was near empty but for a few citizens who were walking the boardwalks.

There were a couple of buckboards over by the Dinsmore Mercantile. One buckboard was being ladened with fresh cut lumber. A couple of horsemen rode the street. At the sheriff's office as they passed by was the sheriff of Rush Springs tacking a few wanted posters to a tack board with the butt of his gun. A few horses were tethered to the hitching rack in front of the Saunders Assay Office next to the bank of Rush Springs. As Walt, Will, and Fletcher reined in at the Chestnut saloon, the silence was broken by gunfire. Walt, Will, and Fletcher turned abruptly towards the gunfire. Suddenly, the door to the bank opened and three men came rushing out from inside, and running to their horses to make their escape. As the robbers tried to mount dancing horses one outlaw had been shot dead in the street. They finally mounted their horses they made a mad dash for safety. A man came running from the bank shouting that the bank was being robbed. He was shot dead on the boardwalk.

Men came running from every direction firing at the bank robbers, The sheriff had come running with his weapon at the ready. As the robbers passed the Chestnut saloon, they looked at Walt, Will, and Fletcher. One man smiled and touched the brim of his hat as they passed.

Will pointed, then said, "Uh, ain't that Creel?" He chuckled.

Walt remarked, "Stop pointing, Will. These people will think we're a part of the gang that robbed the bank." Chuckling, "They robbed the bank. In broad daylight. Gutsy."

Fletcher turned to the direction of the dead man asking, "I wonder who was shot?"

Both Walt and Will turned towards the bank, and the Assay office where the dead man lay in the street. Soon, a crowd of men gathered around the dead man.

The doctor was called for and he came running from his office. People entered the bank to find the vault opened and all their money gone. The bank teller was also shot and killed inside the bank. Women were sobbing over the deaths of the bank manager and the bank teller. It was believed by Walt, Will, and Fletcher they were wives, or daughters of those men, or they were somehow related.

Walt, then said, "Well, let's get mounted."

Fletcher asked, "Why?"

"Creel is the reason we're here ain't it? Let's find 'em before a posse does."

Will, then said, "You really think these people can form a posse? I don't think they can chase and catch a mangey coyote."

Walt turned to Will asking, "Now, why would anybody want to chase and catch a mangey coyote?"

Will turned abruptly to Walt saying, "Oh, be quiet."

Walt chuckled, then said, "Let's get mounted."

Fletcher was peering over the swinging doors, looking into the Chestnut saloon.

He licked his lips, then said, "Hey, Walt? How 'bout a beer? A beer won't hurt, will it? 'Sides it feels like I'm chewin' on cotton."

Will replied, "I agree. I don't think we have anything to worry 'bout. I doubt these hicks can raise up a posse."

Walt looked a little skeptical, but he then relented, "Well, I suppose a beer won't hurt."

Will grinned wide, slapped Fletcher on the arm, and then, they entered the Chestnut saloon. As they entered the saloon, they noticed that the saloon was near empty except for the bartender behind the bar.

The bartender wiped down the bar with a bar towel. He smiled as they walked up.

The bartender asked, "What'll it be, gentlemen?"

Walt looked around the saloon at so many empty tables and chairs. He shook his head slowly. He, turned to the bartender saying, "It's kind a dim and dreary in here ain't it?"

Interested, the bartender asked, "Oh? How so?"

Will scoffed saying, "There are no customers. Is it always like this this time of day?"

The bartender replied, "Yep. The boss likes it that way, plus we never close. We're open seven days a week, even on Sundays. 'Course the men folk don't come in till around ten at night. Plus, we do cater to a few drifters every now and then like yourselves. No offence meant."

Walt said, "None taken. Is 'at a fact huh? Seven days a week?"

The bartender replied, "Sure is. So, what can I get for you fellas?"

Walt said, "Beers all around, Barkeep."

The bartender replied, "Comin' right up."

The bartender grabbed three beer glasses, then filled them from the beer dispenser, then sat them

down on the bar in front of his customers.

He smiled, saying, "There ya are gentlemen. Enjoy."

Fletcher, then said, "This boss of yours, he a slave driver makin' you stay open six days a week, plus on Sunday?"

"Naw, I don't think so. The name's, Higgins. Marty Higgins. I'm the boss. I own the place."

Walt turned to Will saying, "He's the boss."

Will turned to Fletcher saying, "He's the boss." Fletcher replied, "I got that. Thanks."

Will turned back to Walt saying, "He said, thanks."

Walt, then said, "I heard that."

Marty chuckled at the jocularity, then asked, "So, what was all that ruckus out on the street a minute ago? I heard shootin'."

Will said, "There was a lot of shootin'. Three men are dead."

Marty, then asked, "Do you know who it was got killed?"

Walt said, "You don't look all that concerned about what went on out there. Why is that? Ain't you in'trested in any way to just take a look at the goin's on around you?"

"Me? Naw." Marty answered. "See this scar on my cheek? That's what I got the last time I got nosey and poked my nose outside. So, what happened out there?"

Walt answered, "The bank was robbed and we believe the bank manager was killed." Fletcher, then said,

"Also, the bank teller was killed inside the bank, and one of the men who robbed the bank was also killed tryin' to make his getaway."

Marty replied, "Do tell? Ugh, ugh, ugh, such goin's on."

Walt asked, "You don't seem too concerned 'bout the bank bein' robbed? All that money stolen. I hope you didn't lose very much money."

"None of it mine." Marty replied. "I have my money locked away in a secret, and safe place, and I have the only key, though I do feel sorry for those who lost all their money."

Fletcher, then said, "You know, Higgins, some businesses will go under without that money. They stored that money as a nest egg for later use, not to mention the regular citizens in town. So, in essence, that bank robbery will affect your business because they will no longer be your customers. No customers, no money comin' in."

Marty replied, "Why worry 'bout somethin' you have no control over?"

Walt drank down the last dregs of his beer, then said, "Well, shall we?"

Will, and Fletcher did likewise with their beer. The, all three men stood and went to the swinging doors.

Marty smiled, then said, "Come again, gentlemen, if you're back in the area."

When they reached the swinging doors, they stopped, then Walt turned back to Marty.

Walt asked, "Ever hear of a man called Jack Hardee? Or, maybe, Rafe Peterson and Shane Garraty? Ever hear of them?"

"Yes." Marty answered. "I heard of them. Who hasn't. Those men are real mad men. I like to stay away from men like that."

All three men at the saloon doors looked at each other as they laughed a little.

Will, then said, "How do you do that, Mister Higgons, when you cater to such men?"

Marty answered, "I may serve them whiskey and beer, and hopefully a good time, but that is as far as I go.

That's how I make my living. What I don't know won't get me killed."

Fletcher said, "You call this a good time?"

Will, then said, "Yeah. What gives?"

"This?" Marty asked. "Not in the least, but if you're here, say 'round seven o'clock tonight, you'll see this place full of dancin' girls that'll sashay your cares away."

Fletcher grinned a wide grin, then said, "That sounds like a hot-diggety dog of a good time."

Both Walt and Will turned to Fletcher laughing.

Walt saying, "A hot-diggety dog of a good time? Are you serious?"

Will said, "I have never heard you say that."

Fletcher replied, "Never before had a reason to."

Will said, "I'll have to remember that sayin'. Don't care who you are, that's funny."

Marty said, "Oh, by the way, gentlemen, should I see the friends you spoke of, I'll let them know you're lookin' for 'em."

Before going through the swinging doors, Walt replied, "Thanks, Mister Higgins. We appreciate that."

Then there was the whooshing sound of the swinging doors, flapping back and forth. As the men and women of Rush Springs were still out on the street talking about the bank robbery, and the death of the bank manager, the bank teller, and the outlaw bandit, the three men went to their horses, stepped into the stirrups and the swung themselves onto their saddles. They, then reined their horses away from the saloon, and nosed them in the direction following Creel and company when they left town. Kicking their horses in the flanks, they rode at a canter on their way out of town. They were going in search of a man called, Creel, along with a man called, Jon Nagle, and the man from New Orleans, Thadeus Doucet, also known as the man of many ladies.

When Richard Siringo, the patriarch of the Siringo family was put to rest in the family cemetery, women were sobbing, and at times wailing from Mae as well as Jennifer. Tears crowded the eyes of Slim as he stared at the flower strewn casket containing the father he knew his whole life and the man he has loved in the same amount of time. There was sniffling, and tears from a few women who were in attendance. A few people from other ranches and farms showed up at Richard's funeral to pay their last respects. Richard was a well-respected man who demanded respect in his actions as well as in his given word. He was a friend to all and an enemy to none except for Devlin Wade, the self-appointed king of Comanche, Oklahoma. Among the mourners was the Homestead crew. The service was performed by the Reverand, Joseph E. Patterson of the Methodist Church. The only church in Comanche at the time. Tim Rose, the mortician, was in attendance along with four men who were under obligated pay to lower the casket and fill in the grave. They were standing a little ways off from the funeral party during the services. However, after the services, and the ladies had been led away from the cemetery, slumped forward and weeping, Slim walked over to talk to Tim Rose. After a minute of words being said in whispered tones, they exchanged pleasantries, then Tim nodded his head as Slim handed him something. Tim went and paid the four men their obligated pay, and told they were no longer needed. The four men looked at each other dumbfounded, but they somehow understood, so, they turned and left the cemetery. Slim, Mike Eagan, Ross Chambers, Victor Corman, and Morgan Tuttle, owner of the circle T ranch. Jesse Crandall, foreman of the Circle T Ranch accompanied his boss to the funeral.

Chapter Two

That's What They Do

Slim, then went and thanked the Reverand Joeseph E. Patterson for his services, and with sleight of hand, Slim slipped him his pay while they exchanged pleasantries. When the Reverand, Joseph E. Patterson turned and left the cemetery, Morgan Tuttle, Jesse Crandall, Mike Eagan, Victor Corman, and Ross Chambers along with the Homestead crew, stood looking at Slim, unsure of what they should do.

Ross then said, "We'll do what's needs done, Slim. You go comfort your family, and grieve your loss for yourself."

Slim replied, "Thanks, Ross. I appreciate that. I do."

Victor, Ross, Morgan, and Jesse grabbed the ropes on each side of the casket as Mike pulled away the supports. They lowered the casket into the grave to the one foot support at the bottom of the grave to allow retrieval of the ropes from the grave.

Slim stood by and watched as this took place. His face had no expression. Then, to everyone's surprise, he picked up the round headed spade and shoved it into the mound of dirt, and brought up a shovel full. He held the shovel full of dirt over the grave, then turned the shovel over to the right, emptying the shovel full of dirt into the grave. The dirt landed on top of the casket with the sound it made as it landed on the wood of his dad's casket.

Ross said, "Slim, don't. We'll do this."

Slim turned and shoved the spade blade into the mound of dirt. He stared at it for a few seconds.

He then said, "I'm done. Ross. Sorry, but I had the need to do that. The Parson did a great service. Thank you, Gentlemen, for bein' here."

As Slim turned and was leaving the cemetery, Ross, and Morgan picked up the shovels and started filling in the grave. Sound that made echoed in Slim's ears.

Jesse said, "He's standin' perty good for the shape he's in."

Mike said, "He'll soon fall apart, and when he does, he'll have a tough time of it. I don't want to be around him when he does. I just hate to see a growed man cry."

Morgan stopped shoveling, then said, "Like father, like son, they say. Richard sired a young look-alike. Takes after Richard in the right way. His influence in this country will be sorely missed."

Mike, then said, "He had a level head on his shoulders for sure. Good with numbers too."

Victor said, "He sure was nobody's fool, let me tell you. His thinkin' was straight."

Silence fell on the group like a blanket. It took a while, but the grave was finally shoveled in. The silence was broken by an eagle making itself known. Every one of the men in the cemetery looked up at the eagle with its shrill voice.

It mouthed off, letting them know it was there, wings spread wide, soaring low in the sky. It was then they knew Richard Siringo was free.

Jamie, then said, "There are three wounded men in the wagon, Lieutenant. Do you need to know the names, Sir?"

"No, Lieutenant, I don't. They are not my duty, Sir. It is Lieutenant Lundstrom and yours, Sir."

Jamie replied, "Yes, Sir."

Lieutenant Chapman asked, "How is your head wound, Lieutenant? Less dizzy? Getting better I hope."

Jamie smiled, then answered, "Better every day, Lieutenant. Thank you."

Lieutenant Chapman then said, "I assume, due to their wounds, they are unable to sit a horse, but are they able to arm themselves?"

Jamie answered, "Yes, Sir. They were armed during this action."

Captain Locke said, "I suggest they stay armed, Lieutenant. There are more than the Apache on the prod in this area."

Both Jamie and Lieutenant Lundstrom replied, "Yes, Sir."

Both men looked at each other as Captain Locke said, "1st Lieutenant Lundstrom is in command of this detail, Lieutenant Carlson. It will serve you well to remember that, Sir."

Jamie replied, "Yes, Sir. I do, Sir."

Captain Locke then added, "But, I do commend you, Sir, for a job well done. You handled this detail in the greatest principle of the US Cavalry, and in the tradition of a well- disciplined line officer in spite of being wounded yourself."

Jamie replied, "Again, I thank the captain."

Captain Locke, Lieutenant Chapman, Lieutenant Lundstrom and Jamie rode to the wounded wagon. As Captain Locke got even with the wagon seat, he looked up to see the expression on Lieutenant Adam Murtaugh's face. It was sheer delight, masked in sheer terror.

Captain Locke asked Private Ellsworth, "What's wrong with Lieutenant Murtaugh, Private?"

"I believe his mind is gone, Captain," Ellsworth replied. "Since he heard the warbling war cries of those

Apache his mind twisted. He certainly ain't himself, Sir. All he seems to do now is just mumble incoherently."

Captain Locke looked across the horses to Lieutenant Lundstrom saying, "It seems you have another casualty, Lieutenant."

Lieutenant Lundstrom sat his horse staring at 2nd Lieutenant Adam Murtaugh in disbelief, then he sighed heavily with a sneer on his face.

Captain Locke then said, "Take care of the lieutenant, Private. Even though his mind is gone, he is still an officer in the United States Cavalry."

Private Ellsworth replied, "Sure thing, Captain. With kid gloves, Sir."

Captain Locke then said, "Your wagon will be first in line, Lieutenant Lundstrom. That way, when we separate a few miles from here, our wagons can veer off to the southwest while your wagon continues on its journey west to Ringgold Barracks."

Lieutenant Lundstrom replied, "Yes, Sir."

Lieutenant Lundstrom looked up at the box and saw no one there. He looked at Captain Locke who, then said, "Whenever you're ready, Lieutenant."

Lieutenant Lundstrom replied, "Yes, Sir." He turned saying, "Give the private a hand, Corporal Sande, then be ready to move out."

Corporal Sande replied, "Yes, Sir."

Corporal Sande dismounted, climbed up into the wagon from the rear gate, and assisted Private Ellsworth with Lieutenant Murtaugh and his comfort. They laid the lieutenant down and covered him with a blanket, which he grasped quite readily with a faraway look, and fear.

Private Ernie Post remarked, "The Apache never touched him, and still, they killed him."

Private Fairfield added, "That's too bad. He looked as though was doin' just fine. Now, look at him. A shriveled up piece of what used to be."

When Private Ellsworth had taken his place on the wagon seat, and Corporal Sande had

mounted his horse, the lieutenant took notice.

Lieutenant Lundstrom rode to the side of the wagon saying, "Move out, Private."

Private Ellsworth yelled out as he slapped the reins over the horses' back, "Yee-hah! Yee-hah! Get up there!"

Captain Locke, then hollered, "Move out!"

Then, the column of wagons moved out, slow, but sure. Then Captain Locke reined his horse to a halt, and when scout, Ned Grayson came up to him, he kicked his horse in the flanks to ride beside Grayson. Captain Locke suggested that Grayson do what he was getting paid to do. Then, Ned slapped the reins on the rump of his horse, and took off to the front of the column.

1st Lieutenant Chapman rode up beside Captain Locke saying, "Persnickety ol' cuss ain't he, Captain?"

Captain Locke chuckled replying, "He is that, Mister Chapman, but I hear he's one of the best the Army has, so treat him kindly."

Chuckling, Lieutenant Chapman replied, "Yes, Sir."

The column of wagons moved on, until within the hour, the column came to a halt. Captain Locke,

Lieutenant Chapman, Lieutenant Lundstrom and Jamie rode out to where Ned Grayson sat his horse, unmoving. As the four men rode to where Grayson was, each man wondered why was he just sitting there. When they approached Grayson, they couldn't see what he was looking at. When they got to him, he motioned with his head to look over the embankment. Halfway down a 20 foot embankment lay the body of Private Hugh McCracken. He had at least two arrows in him.

Captain Locke hollered back to the column, "Sergeant Ralston!"

Ned said, "No need, Captain. Those arrows are Caddo arrows. He hasn't been dead long. A couple hours, maybe less. He put up a good fight, I'll say that for him. He held them off for a couple hours, or more, according to the signs I see." He surveyed the area, then said, "They could still be lurking in the area."

Lieutenant Chapman, then asked, "I wonder if Private Streat made it?"

The captain quickly turned to look at Lieutenant Chapman then slightly shook his head.

He breathed deep, exhaled, then said, "I wish I knew, Lieutenant. I wish I knew."

Ned, then asked, "There's another trooper out here somewhere?"

The captain replied, "Yes. I sent two gallopers to Fort Richardson after we had been attacked by Kiowa, requesting re-enforcements. Private Streat was sent out before Private McCracken. Five minutes apart. My reasoning was two is better than one."

"So, what was this troopers name?"

Captain Locke answered, "Unfortunately, that was Hugh McCracken. I hope Streat hasn't met with the same fate, if so, no re-enforcements." He turned in his saddle yelling, "Sergeant Ralston, McCracken, dead man."

Sergeant 1st Class, Gene Ralston replied, "Yes, Sir."

Captain Locke, then said, "Find a place for him somewhere, Sergeant, and be quick about it."

Sergeant Ralston replied, "Yes, Sir."

The captain added, "We need to move and move fast. Understood?"

Sergeant Ralston replied, "Yes, Sir. I understand, Captain." He turned in the saddle and hollered, "Privates, Covington, and Epps. McCracken, dead man. Find a spot for him."

Brett Covington turned to Tom Epps saying, "Find a spot for him he says." Scoffs, "I don't believe McCracken would care where we put him. Do you, Tom?"

Tom Epps replied, "Not in the least, Brett, but orders is orders."

Without a word to the sergeant, the two privates dismounted and went to the body of Hugh McCracken on the downhill side of the embankment.

Picking the body up, they struggled to get the body to the top of the embankment.

When they finally did, they were out of breath.

Sergeant Ralston, then said, "Travers, Kellerman, you two help them with the body. Now, get in there and lend a hand."

Both Privates, Ed Travers and John Kellerman quickly jumped in and helped pick up the lifeless body of Hugh McCracken.

They carried the body to a wagon for the dead, then they put the body on the wagon. In a little over fifteen minutes the column was again on the move. Army scout, Ned Grayson reined his horse away from the column to scout far ahead, while Sergeant Major, Del Dickerson decided to take the point well ahead of the column. Ever on the alert for attack from Indians such as the Kiowa, Apache, Caddo, or Comanche was nerve wracking. Every man jack of them had nervous anxiety, nausea, fear, causing each man to be stressed out. There was very little to say from anyone, so very little was said by anyone.

It was well after eight o'clock in the morning when Karl Stokes and Paul Stroud finally entered the Lucky Deuce Saloon where Devlin Wade waited on news of last night's raid on the Silver Shovel silver mine in an attempt to get the signatures of Amos Stegner and Seth Brubaker, owners of said mine to sign the deed of transfer over to Wade. When Wade seen Larry and Cecil come in the saloon, he motioned with his head to have them go to his office. Wade sat his whiskey glass down on the bar, then stepped away from it going to his office. When he got to his office, he found them waiting for him outside.

Wade opened the door saying, "Get in here. Both a ya."

As both men entered Wade's office, the look he gave them caused them to flinch without getting punched.

When Wade slammed the door behind him, he said, "How dare you keep me waiting. I should fire you! Better yet, have you shot!"

Karl said, "You wouldn't do that, would you, Boss? Have us shot, I mean."

"Why wouldn't I?" Wade snapped back. "Why…?" He calmed himself as he rubbed the back of his neck, then asked, "Why did you kill Amos Stegner? I needed his signature on that deed transfer, you nit-wits."

Paul replied, "He gave us no other choice, Wade. They shot at us, so, naturally we shot back."

Wade, then said, "They? I hear you never seen hide nor hair of Seth Brubaker. You simply ran him out a the country."

Karl replied, "Say, that's right. Then, your takeover of the mine is in the bag. Wade looked at him out of curiosity, then asked, "How do you figure that?"

Karl answered, "With one man dead, and the other man out a the country, there's no one to contest your claim to it."

Paul said, "Yeah." He smiled, then said, "It's like it worked itself out in your favor."

Without saying a word, Wade stepped over to the window as Cecil and Larry congratulated each other silently for coming up with that explanation. Wade looked out the window, but stared out into nothing as he mulled that statement over in his head.

After a few seconds with no reply, Karl asked, "You alright, Boss?"

Paul said, "Yeah. You're awfully quiet when you were in such a dither before."

Wade turned from the window saying, "I was ready to strangle you two, you do know that? Or, have you both shot, but what you say is very true. It did work out for the best for me. I believe what happened was pure dumb luck. Yes, sir, pure dumb luck. Why, there's not a court in the land that would take that mine from me. Not now. No way." scoffs "Not under these circumstances it wouldn't."

Karl, then asked, "So, you're not mad at us anymore?"

Wade smiled then replied, "Oh, I'm still mad, but I'm slowly getting over that."

Paul said, "That's good to hear, Boss. The reason we was late was because we had breakfast at the diner, and they was rather busy."

Wade replied, "You were lucky, but do me a favor. Don't keep me waitin' ever again."

Karl replied, "That's not a problem, Boss"

Paul, then remarked, "Yeah, what he said, Wade."

Wade, then said, "That's good. That's real good. I'm not so much in a dither, as you so aptly put it, Paul, as I once was. Actually, I am becoming more and more light hearted 'bout the whole cockeyed thing."

Karl asked, "Does that mean we're back in your good graces?"

Through his chuckling, Wade replied, "Yes, yes. Now, get out a here. Both a ya. Go have a liquid breakfast."

Paul said, "We already had breakfast, Boss."

Wade answered, "Oh, that's right. You did, didn't you? Well, still, enjoy the day."

Paul replied, "Thanks, Boss." He smiled.

Smiling graciously, Karl said, "Yeah, thanks, Wade."

Smiling, Wade replied, "No problem, Gentlemen. Have a good day."

Karl and Paul left Wade's office and entered the main room of the saloon. They sauntered up to the bar and ordered a bottle of whiskey and two glasses.

Karl said, "Let's find a table and celebrate."

Paul asked, "Good idea. What will we celebrate?"

As the two sat down at a table, Karl replied, "Wade is no longer mad at us for killin' that miner, Amos Stegner. It all worked out for the best. How's that for a reason to celebrate?"

Paul, then remarked, "That does ring some merit, don't it?"

Karl, then said, "I wonder if one bottle will do us in our celebration?"

Paul answered, "I'll get another one." Turning to the bar, Paul hollered, "Hey, Fred? Let's have another bottle over here. We're celebratin'."

Fred Eubanks, the bartender took another bottle of whiskey over to the table. As he sat the bottle down, he asked joyfully, "So, fellas? What are you celebratin'?"

Paul replied, "Because we did a good job last night."

Karl, then said, "And, Wade is a happy man for it."

"May I join the celebration?" Fred asked.

Karl looked up at Fred, asking, "Were you there last night?"

Fred replied sheepishly, "Well, no…"

Karl looked at Paul, then back at Fred saying, "Get lost."

Fred looked at both men with daggers in his eyes, then turned away from the table.

Paul said, "You handled that with finesse."

Karl replied, "Thank you."

Paul pulled the cork on the first bottle of whiskey, then poured himself three fingers of whiskey, then waited for Karl to do the same. They touched glasses in a salute.

Karl, then said, "Here's to a successful night's work."

Paul, then replied, "Here, here."

Then, both men swallowed the brown fiery liquid in one gulp. As the whiskey burned their throat, they both soured their faces as the whiskey coated their mouth and tongues.

Mary asked enthusiastically, "You want to hold your Godson, Matt?"

Matt took a step back, turned to Reggie who just smiled back at him.

He turned back to Mary saying, "Who? Me? Hold my… him? Aw no. I don't think so, Mary. He's so small, and so… small. I might drop him, or hurt him in some way, so no, I, I, I."

Mary asked, "You sure? He's light as a feather."

Matt replied cautiously, "I'll lay odds the feather outweighs him." Matt began to sidestep along the edge of the bed, saying, "Well, folks, I 'spect I best be goin'. Thanks again for makin' me his godfather 'n all. I sure do appreciate that." As he rounded the foot of the bed, he said, "Well, it sure was nice seein' folks you again. I'll come back sometime in the next few days." When Matt came to the door, he opened it, then said, "Well, see ya."

The door quickly closed behind him and latched.

Confused, Reggie stared at the closed door saying, "See. I told you he'd be ecstatic."

Then, the front door opened and latched when it closed.

Mary replied, "More like scared to death, if you ask me. Poor thing."

Reggie chuckled, then said, "I wonder if he took his horse?"

Then, both Mary and Reggie heard the pounding of horses' hooves going away from the house.

Mary, then replied, "It sounds like he did, Reggie." Mary smiled up at Reggie asking, "Can I impose on you, Reg?"
Reggie answered, "Of course you can. What is it?"

Mary said, "I am a tad bit hungry. I could use a bite to eat. What meat do we have left in the kitchen? I sure could use a sandwich, if you wouldn't mind."

When Matt left Reggie and Mary Carver, he thought of just nosing Shadow south and leaving Duncan to go back to the Homestead near Comanche, but something told him to check in at the telegraph office. Reason? There may be an answer from Cynthia Hickman, Greg Hickman's sister out of Blufton, Indiana. It must have been a real hard blow to her when she received a telegram from someone she never knew letting her know that her brother was dead, when and where and how he died. When he entered the telegraph office, Earl Toliver, the telegraph operator, stood, then stepped away from the telegraph keys. He turned to see Matt coming in the door.

Earl said, "Sheriff, you saved me from havin' to go lookin' for you."

"Oh?" Matt asked.

"Yeah." Earl said. "It seems that message you sent to a, Cynthia Hickman, well, she has sent you a reply."

Earl handed the message to Matt who then read it. When he finished reading it, he looked unfazed by it, yet, he folded it, and then put it in his inside vest pocket.

Matt turned and opened the door, then turned back saying, "Thanks, Earl. I appreciate it."

Earl answered, "Anytime, Sheriff. Anytime."

Matt left the telegraph office, untethered Shadow from the hitching rack, then mounted. Pulling the reins tighter to him, he reined Shadow away from the telegraph office and headed out of town. He nosed Shadow south towards Comanche and the Homestead. He was carrying some important information with him as he trotted out of Duncan, going straight south to Homestead.

The road was easy and unhindered. He smiled as he rode along, knowing he had information written on paper, and it was tucked away inside his vest pocket. He could hardly wait to tell everyone what that information is. He got a little hurried in his want to tell them, so much so, that he picked up the pace. He brought Shadow to a lope and rode on. He knew he was coming up to the turnoff to the Homestead. The turn off heading east to the Homestead ranch was close to two miles away from his present position going south. Then five miles to the Homestead ranch itself. He figured he should be at the Homestead in no time at all. He had not a worry on his mind this day, until he heard the shrill, warbling war cry from Indians. He abruptly turned in the direction of where the war cries were coming from. He saw ten to twelve Indian braves screaming and yelling, and loud enough to raise the dead charging at him. He hastily kicked Shadow in the flanks and Shadow came to near full gallop almost at the outset. As Matt raced along the southbound road to the Homestead, he turned his head to look back at the Indians chasing him. Caddo Indian war party. He crouched forwards over the saddle to become less of a target. He rode hard in his effort to escape the Indian attack. He, then realized he couldn't lead these Indians to the Homestead, so he decided to race into Comanche, hoping the Indians would follow him, and Wade's gunmen would target them, and not him. He would find a hiding place somewhere along the road while the shooting war in Comanche started. He smiled at the idea of giving Wade another worry, Indians. Ha, ha, ha. Caddo at that. But, first, he had to outrun them, then lead them into the town of Comanche. He slapped leather all along the south road, with the screaming Caddo trying their best to catch him.

It wasn't long until the town of Comanche came into view. The Caddo Indian war party seemed to be unaware of where they were in their zeal to catch and kill this white man. As he rounded a curve in the road, he was temporarily out of sight of the Caddo war party due to trees on the side of the road. He quickly reined Shadow into a stand of trees with high brush and low hanging limbs. He watched as the Indians passed as they headed in a hurry towards the town of Comanche screaming and yelling as they went by. At that point, he had a thought, which brought out a snicker from him. The thought was, 'wouldn't it have been funny if it was a war party of Comanche racing towards the town of Comanche'? As luck would have it, there was a man on a spring wagon headed for Comanche. He was near the entrance of Comanche when the Caddo came upon him. He slapped the reins and started yelling about the Indians. As the man raced into Comanche, the Indians pulled up short. A few of Wade's men took cover and the people on the boardwalks ran for cover. A few shots rang out towards the Indians, who then returned fire. The gunshots lasted for another minute or so, from both sides. As the Indians sat on dancing horses, they took their potshots whenever it became available for them to do so.

Then, the Caddo turned and raced away. No one was hurt on either side. The Caddo didn't use the main road when they left. They took off cross country screaming and yelling their warbling war cry as the left. Wade had come from the saloon wondering what the shooting, shouting was all about.

A man standing by the swinging doors said, "Indians, Boss."

Wade replied, "Indians? You sure, Mark?"

Mark answered, "Yes, Sir." pointing "They was chasin' that feller there who was drivin' the spring wagon. He dang near brought those cutthroats all the way into town."

Turning to the man, Wade, then said, "Really? Well, let's just find out why he was bein' chased."

Scoffing, Mark replied, "They was Injuns, Wade. That's what they do."

Ignoring Mark's response, Wade and Mark Crocker walked over to the man who had been driving the spring wagon, but was now hiding behind a 90 gallon water barrel. The man was so afraid; he was visibly shaking from fright. Wade's men who drove off the Indians started to come from their places of cover, one, two at a time. At that same time, Matt reined Shadow out from the protection of the trees and high brush back onto the main road. Matt then nosed Shadow north on the main road to the fork, going east to the Homestead. He rode hard to the east turnoff, which was a few miles north from where he was. He reined Shadow onto the east turnoff with no decline in speed.

As Mike Eagan, Victor Corman, Ross Chambers, Morgan Tuttle of the circle T ranch, and his foreman, Jesse Crandall were staring at the eagle in the sky making itself known with its shrill cry, Matt came galloping into the courtyard of the Homestead. Matt reined Shadow over to the corral, stepped down from the saddle and tethered Shadow to the center rail. By the time the men in the cemetery had come to the courtyard, Slim had come from the house.

Slim said, "Well, look who decided to show up."

Matt, then asked, "Who's that?"

Slim replied, "You, you dumb cluck."

Matt, then said, "Oh, ha, ha, ha. You ain't funny."

Slim asked, "You have any trouble?"

Matt replied, "Yeah. A Caddo Indian war party. They chased me a few miles, then I led them into Comanche. I thought that might give Wade somethin' else to worry 'bout."

The men who were there chuckled as Slim said, "I bet that made him happy."

Matt, then said, "I wouldn't know. I was too busy stayin' still in a stand a trees alongside of the road, but I heard Wade's gunmen, and the Caddo exchanged gunfire. Wade's gunmen finally chased the war party away, and the Indians took off cross country. I took to the main road and backtracked, to the east turnoff to come here to the Homestead."

Slim, then said, "Glad you're all right, Sheriff. I take it you sent that telegram to Greg's sister, what's her name?"

Matt answered, "I did, and I received a reply from Cynthia Hickman from Blufton, Indiana. I have it here."

Matt took the telegram from his inside vest pocket and handed it to Slim. Slim read the telegram. The other men stood by waiting to hear the news.

When Slim had finished reading the telegram, he smiled, then said, "Well, fellas, it sounds as if Cynthia Hickman is comin' to Comanche. She should be here in a couple weeks, so the message says. As soon as she can book passage on the next westbound stage, she'll be on her way here."

Mike, then said, "Jumpin' Jehosaphat! She's headin' into a hornet's nest by comin' here. Why on earth would she do such a thing?"

Slim replied, "I would think that would be obvious, Mike. She's comin' to get some degree of closure after the death of her brother."

Chapter Three

A Difficult Road

Ross, then asked, "I wonder if she's perty?"

Slim answered, "She's a married woman, Ross."

Ross scoffed, then said, "Yeah, well, there's that."

Morgan said, "Well, Jesse, I figure it's time we leave these fine folks to themselves. We have a long day ahead of us tomorrow. It is branding season, and we have yearlings to brand."

Jesse replied, "It'll be a long day for sure."

As Slim, Morgan, and Jesse exchange pleasantries, Slim said, "Thanks for comin', Morg. It means a lot to me, well, to the family actually."

Morgan replied, "I'm glad I could be of support to you, and Mae, and Jenny, Danny. You're good people, and Richard… well, he was a hell of a man, and a good friend, but, I'm not tellin' you somethin' you don't already know, am I?"

"No Morgan, you're not," Slim replied. "but it is good to hear you believe that. Thank you."

Morgan nodded, then turned to Jesse saying, "Whenever you're ready, Jess."

Jesse replied, "Be right with ya, Mister Tuttle" Turning back to Slim, he said, "I am sorry for your loss, Danny. I didn't know your dad all that well, but, from what I've heard it was a lot of good things. My condolences to you and your family."

Slim answered, "Thanks, Jesse. I, we appreciate that."

At the same time, there came a clamor of sorry's, and voices of condolences from the crew of the Homestead. Then Morgan, Jesse, and the crew of the Homestead left the cemetery. They mounted their horses and rode away.

The only ones left in the courtyard was Ross Chambers, Mike Eagan, Victor Corman, Sheriff Matt Tucker, and of course, Slim.

Everyone turned towards the house when they heard the front door open and close. Out of the house came Jenny, sniffling into a hanky as she walked.

When she had reached Slim and the rest, Slim asked, "How's Mom, Jenny?"

Jenny answered, "Not too well, as you might expect." Slim asked, "Then, why ain't you in there with her?"

Jenny replied, "She's asleep in her room, so, I thought I'd come out and visit with you fellas."

Looking somewhat interested, she asked, "So, I'd like to thank you boys for comin'. So, what's up?"

Slim replied, "We received a telegram today from the sister of Grag Hickman…"

Jenny butted in saying, "Now, ain't that nice. His sister is comin' to see him."

Slim went on saying, "who was killed yesterday. She's comin' here from Blufton, Indiana to see her brother's grave and gain closure."

The knowledge that Greg Hickman was dead took her breath away. So much so, she then gasped.

Placing her hands to her chest, Jenny said, "I had no idea that Greg was dead. He was such a kind man. How did he die, and when did he die?"

Victor Corman supplied the answers by saying, "He died in a cattle stampede. They were bein' rustled by what we believe is Wade's gunmen yesterday."

Surprised, she asked, "Yesterday?" She, then said, "Greg can't be above ground for two weeks waitin' for his sister to show up. That ain't decent."

Slim said, "Now, Jenny, don't go gettin' your dander up. He's already below ground. We buried him yesterday."

Ross, then said, "So, don't worry, Jenny. There's nothin' to worry 'bout. Is there, Slim?"

Slim replied, "Well, I don't know, Ross." Turning to Matt, he asked, "She does know that, doesn't she, Matt?"

Matt scoffed, then said, "Why, of course she knows that." He scoffs again, asking, "She does need to know that, ya know?"

Slim said, "Yeah, I know."

Matt, then said, "So, I told her, her brother had been buried."

Jenny, then said, "It's good she knows so there is no misunderstanding." She smiled, then said, "So, we're expectin' company from, where did you say, Danny?"

Slim answered. "Cynthia Hickman out of Blufton, Indiana."

Jenny reiterated saying, "Cynthia Hickman. Nice name. She married?"

Slim said, "Yeah, she's married, Jen, but, we have no idea what her married name is."

Matt said, "I sent it to the only name we knew in hopes we got it to the right person, and evidently, we did."

Jenny said, "Hmm, makes you wonder if her husband will make that trip with her?"

Matt replied, "We'll know that when she gets here, but to keep her, or them both safe, we'll need to stop that stage long before it reaches Comanche. They just may become a target for Wade's reprisal when he himself finds out who they are."

Slim had a faraway look on his face. Jenny, and the others noticed it. It bothered Jenny to the point of being puzzled.

Jenny, then asked, "What's the matter, Danny? Why the long face?"

Slim took a deep breath, then replied, "Just wonderin', Jenny."

Jenny asked, "About?"

Slim answered, "Just wondering where Walt, Will, and Fletcher could be. We sure could use them right 'bout now."

Jenny asked, "You don't suppose they ran out on us, do ya?"

Slim replied, "They're not the kind of men to do that, Jenny, but there must be a reason for their absence. I'm just tryin' to figure out just what that reason is."

Ross, then spoke saying, "The men I know would not leave you holdin' the bag. They were stout, true to their word kind a men. I wouldn't worry too much 'bout them. They could be up to somethin' we have no idea 'bout."

Slim replied, "I'm not worried, Ross. I just haven't got the fain'test idea as to where they went, or what they're up to. Why would they just up and leave without sayin' a word?"

Ross, then said, "I wouldn't worry 'bout them, Slim. They'll show up, sooner, or later."

Slim replied, "I know you're right, Ross. Question is, when."

Jenny, then said, "Well, let's not worry 'bout that right now. Let's go in the house and have a cup a coffee."

Mike said, "No coffee for me, thanks. That would be interruptin' your time of grief, and I'll not do that."

Ross, then said, "I found when you worry 'bout somethin' you have no control over it can give you unnecessary anxiety, and a nervous indigestion."

Walt Gratton, Fletcher Sullivan and Will Ferguson left the town of Rush Springs,

Oklahoma, and they left at full gallop. They slapped leather chasing after the men who robbed the bank of Rush Springs. Those who robbed the bank were men they knew, and had ridden with, a time, or two. They weren't trying to recover the money that was stolen, or bring the money and the bank robbers back to jail, and then for them to stand trial for murder of the bank manager, and the bank teller. Far from it. They wanted to catch up to them for another reason altogether. They wanted to offer them a proposition in hopes they would listen, and then, take up that offer. It would be considered a favor, and a debt to Walt if they did. The three rode hard tracking the men they were after. They rode for a couple of hours, stopping only to make sure of the tracks they were following. Walt had an idea when they last stopped just where the robbers were going.

He said as much to Will and Fletcher.

Will said, "I know of that cabin. It's an old miner's cabin. It's nestled in the rocks so good you could ride right by it and never see it. You have to be looking for it in order to find it."
Walt, then said, "It's the only place in the area where they could be going. That's where I'd go."

Fletcher asked, "How far is this cabin?"

Walt replied, "A few more miles. Up near Coyote Creek, though the creek itself doesn't flow close to the cabin, but it's only a short walk from it."

Fletcher said, "Well, I know one thing. If we go ridin' in like we own the place, we may get a lead reception with them thinkin' we're the posse."

Walt, then said, "That's true, so, we'll take care not to get that lead reception while we let them know who we are."

A couple hours, or so later they dismounted their horses amongst the boulders and rocks near Coyote Creek and followed it to the cabin. When they got within around fifty yards of the cabin, they stopped, and then, Walt yelled out.

Walt hollered, "Hey, Creel! You there in the cabin! This is Walt Gratton! You remember me?"

From inside the cabin, Creel hollered back, "Yeah, I remember you, Walt! Who else is there with you?"

Will yelled out, "Will Ferguson, Creel! Can we approach the cabin?"

Creel, then hollered, "Who's that other fella there with you, Will? Ain't never seen him afore!"

Will hollered back, "He's a good friend a ours, Creel! His name is Fletcher Sullivan! He's real trustworthy, real handy with a gun, and he's a good man!"

Walt, then said, "Well, seein' as how you know who we are, is Jonas Eberly in there?"

Jonas replied, "I'm in here, Walt. It's good to hear from you again. How you been?"

Walt replied, "Aw, fair to middling, Jonas. You know how it is."

Then, Will asked, "You in there too, Jon Nagle?"

Creel yelled back, "Jon Nagle is dead in Rush Springs! How did you know where to find us, Walt?"

Walt hollered back, "We were in Rush Springs when you fellas robbed the bank! We had just arrived in town, and we was lookin' for you!"

Creel hollered back, "Now, why in thunderation was you lookin' for me, Walt?"

Walt answered, "Well, if we can come in the cabin where we can talk freely…!"

Creel asked, "Anybody else with you?"

Walt replied, "No. It's just us three, Creel."

Creel yelled out, "Well, then, come ahead on! We're friendly!"

Walt, then said, "Thanks, Creel! We appreciate it!"

All three men stood from their cover and started walking cautiously towards the cabin.

Walt yelled out, "We're comin' in, Creel, so, don't none a you shoot! We're friends!"

Inside the cabin was the man called, Creel, Jonas Eberly, and Thaddeus Doucet from Louisiana. Walt never knew Creel's real name. He only knew him as Creel, and right now, at this moment, he was going to the cabin where Creel and his co-horts were.

Creel turned to Jonas Eberly saying, "Get that money off the table, and hide them saddlebags."

Jonas replied, "Why? They already know we have the bank money."

Creel answered, "Because I said so, that's why. Leave no temptation."

Thaddeus Doucet was standing by the window, then spoke in his broken French accent.

Thaddeus said, "Monsieur Creel, do you not trust these fellows comin' to the cabin?"

Creel turned to Thaddeus saying, "I did at one time, but things could have changed since then, so, keep your eyes open. I trust them only so far."

As the door to the cabin opened, Walt, Fletcher and Will, stood back from it on the safe side. They were just out of eyesight, so Creel, Jonas, and Thaddeus stared at the entryway, wondering where the three men went. Creel, confused, stood staring out the opened door. He turned to Thaddeus, and Jonas and they also were perplexed.

Jonas asked, "Where are they?"

Then Creel said, "I don't know. Walt? Where'd you go?"

Then, Walt stood in the doorway.

Creel, then said in a soft, yet restrained tone of voice, "Walt."

Walt smiled as he stood staring at Creel.

Walt then said, "Can't be too careful these days, Creel. You know how it is. Don't take it too serious. No offense meant."

Creel turned to look at Jonas, and Thaddeus, then he turned back to Walt, and began to laugh.

Laughing down to a chuckle, Creel finally said, "Same ol' Walt. Never take nothin' for granted, not even friendship."

Walt replied, "A man can stay alive a little longer that way." He smiled.

Then, Fletcher and Will, showed themselves, and stood to one side behind Walt.

Chuckling, Creel gestured saying, "Come in. Come in my friends."

As Walt, Fletcher and Will entered the cabin, Thaddeus asked, "You brought some whiskey with you, no?"

Will replied, "No, sorry. No whiskey."

Thaddeus, then said, "Aww, what a shame, Monsieur. Ah, se-la-vie."

Will said, "You don't look so dapper, Thaddeus. What happened?"

Thaddeus answered empathetically, "Aww, now, William, you must forgive the discrepancy of my fine linen. Tis the life of an outlaw, no? And, since there is no whiskey, I am twice burdened by the memory of it."

Jonas, then said, "Thad and his fine, uppity words." Thaddeus bows. "So, Walt, what brings you three here?"

Creel said, "That's right, Jonas. Walt, you said somethin' 'bout a proposition? What kind a proposition are you offerin'?"

Walt answered, "Ah, yes, the proposition."

Walt sits at the table, then Creel does the same, but he sits opposite of Walt. Creel, again, says, "Let's have it, Walt. What is the proposition you have for me?"

Walt replied, "Have you ever been to Comanche, Oklahoma, Creel."

Muddled, Creel answered, "I don't believe I ever have."

Thaddeus said, "I have, Monsieur. A quain't little burg, I must say. Have you ever been there?"

Walt answered, "We came from there lookin' for Creel here, and you fellas of course."

Creel asked, "So, what has Comanche, Oklahoma got to do with us?"

Will, then asked, "Have you been there in recent months, Thad?"

"Ah, no, I'm afraid not, William. It has been a few years since I have been in Comanche. But, as Monsieur Creel has asked, what has Comanche, Oklahoma to do with us?"

Walt replied, "Comanche, as well as Stephen's County itself, is being overrun by a man called, Devlin Wade. He has terrorized, and killed whole families, rustled their cattle, grabbed their land, and their property. He's got Comanche so bottled up with his hired guns, nothin' goes in, or out without him knowin' 'bout it. He's been a real hell raiser, and dictator."

Creel, then asked, "A dictator?" Chuckling, "So, what has that have to do with us?"

Fletcher spoke saying, "There are friends of ours who live near Comanche. They own a ranch called Homestead. They've been harassed, and a family member was killed in order to wear down their resistance of that family to sell their property and their holdings over to Wade."

Jonas, then asked, "I don't understand. What does that have to do with us, Walt? Lay your cards out on the table and tell us what's your proposition is?"

Creel said, "It does seem you're goin' the long way 'round the barn to tell us somethin',

so what is it you're tryin' to say?"

Walt looked across the table at Creel who stared intently at him, then smiled.

Walt, then said, "I'd like for you fellas to help me, and my friends in Comanche to get rid of this man Devlin Wade. That's my proposition. I would deem it a great favor on my part."

Creel steadily looked to Jonas, then to Thaddeus. Both men were standing near the window at the front of the cabin, and both men stared at Creel with speculation and suspicion in their eyes. Creel turned his attention back to Walt.

Creel, then said, "A favor, huh? A great favor you say? So, what's in it for us, Walt? I mean, we're all three business men here, so tell us, what will we get if we decide to help you and your friends to get rid of this man Devlin Wade?"

Walt replied, "As I said, a great favor for me, and I'm almost ready to say that my friends will be so happy you're helpin' them, they just may pay you handsomely."

Jonas, then said, "But, you can't guarantee that, can you, Walt?"

Walt answered, "Well, no I can't guarantee that, Jonas, but that's because we left in such a hurry, it didn't even dawn on us, at the time, to ask. Of course, they had no idea we were leavin', or what we'd be doin'."

Creel smiled a crooked smiled, then said, "So, what you're sayin' is, those people have no idea what you're up to?"

Walt answered, "No, they don't. As I said, we left in a hurry." He looked at Creel, then Jonas, and then Thaddeus, then back to Creel, then said, "So, what's your answer, Creel? You fellas willin' to help these folks?" Hesitantly, he added, "But, there is one stipulation, Creel."

"And that is?" Creel asked as he chuckled.

Walt replied, "Once you help get rid of Wade, and his gunmen, you fellas will not try to take over where Wade left off. Agreed?"

Creel answered, "Well, first off, Walt, we never said we'd help get rid of this man Wade, and second, we're not even guaranteed any kind of pay for doin' that. All we have so far is, it will be a great favor to you."

Walt just stared back at him without sayin' a word with eyes of worry.

Then, Creel asked, "What is it that makes you think you deserve this favor from us? Name a time when that happened."

"In all actuality, Creel, I was bankin' on the fact that we're friends." Walt replied. "By the way, speaking of banks, how much did you get away with from the bank in Rush Springs?"

Creel smiled a crooked smiled then said, "Enough to last a few days."

Fletcher then said, "That much, huh?"

Creel looked at Fletcher with distrust, then asked, "Just how do you figure into this scheme of things, Fletcher?"

Fletcher replied, "They're my friends too."

"I should a guessed." Creel said. "So, Walt, when do you need the answer to your proposition, such as it is?"

Walt replied, "The sooner the better, Creel. People are dyin' almost on a daily basis. Wade is gettin' stronger every day. He even designed an assassination of the county sheriff, but we foiled that, and saved the sheriff from bein' killed."

Creel looked at Walt confused, then asked, "Just when have you been worried 'bout how many people are killed, especially a sheriff, who may come lookin' for you because your face is on a wanted poster, or on a circular?"

Walt answered, "True, it could've happened, Creel, but it didn't."

Will then said, "So, what do you say to that?"

Creel then said. "Well, of course it didn't happen. You fellas pulled his fat out a the fire. If that was me, I, myself, would be very happy 'bout that, and I'd even suddenly get amnesia on a few things, if you know what I mean?"

Walt replied, "I see what you mean, but I need to hear what you have to say 'bout what we've discussed as soon as possible. We need to be gettin' back rather quickly."

Thaddeus, then asked, "What if we don't take you up on that proposition, Walter? What would you do then?" Fletcher replied quickly, "We'll go elsewhere."

Jonas asked, "And, do what?"

Walt answered, "We'd go to Texas. Look for Shane Garraty, Jack Hardee, and Rafe Peterson."

Creel, then asked, "And, they are?"

Walt answered, "As I said, in Texas, somewhere near Paducah from what I've heard. A little far to travel, but hopefully a more prosperous ride, and an agreement."

Creel, then said, "Well, we'll need to talk this over, so, if you don't mind waitin' outside while we discuss this proposition of yours that would be great. Oh, first a question."

"What's the question?" Walt asked.

Creel asked, "What are they payin' you for your help?"

Fletcher spoke saying, "Friendship."

Creel, Thaddeus, and Jonas laughed at that while Walt, Fletcher, and Will looked on with quiet resolve.

Creel, talking while chuckling said, "And, you expect us to do the same?"

The laughter continued as Walt stood back from the table.

Walt turned to Will, and Fletcher saying, "Looks like we took a long ride for nothin', Fellas. I'm sorry we couldn't have come to an agreement. So, we'll just mosey on down the road, Creel."

Creel looked at Walt, then said, "Goin' to Texas, huh?"

"Seems to be the way of it." Walt replied.

"We haven't had time to discuss the proposition you offered." Creel said.

"Would it do any good?" Walt asked.

Creel, then said, "You never know. It could turn out in your favor. So, how 'bout it?"

Walt turned to look at Fletcher who shrugged his shoulders. Will did the same when Walt turned to him.

Walt, then said, "Why not? We'll give you a little time for discussion, but, not too much time. Remember, we need to be on our way, either with you, or on our way to Paducah."

As the wagons of the combined forces of Captain, Gary Locke, and 1st Lieutenant, Miles Lundstrom moved along, the troopers continued their vigilant search for danger. Ever on the alert as they rode. Eyes searching every bush, tree, and an outcrop of large boulders. Sweat stung their eyes as the sweat ran down their faces. Metal rang against metal. The sound of horses' hooves that pounded steadily against the soft earth. The rattle, the creaks, moans and groans of the over laden wagons were putting deep wagon ruts in the earth. Drivers of those wagons wore their neckerchiefs over their mouths and noses because the stench of those dead bodies was intense, and overwhelming. So much so, they had to keep changing wagon drivers every hour, or so, as not to have ill and vomiting troopers. Captain Locke sat his horse at the side of the trail and watched the wagons as they passed him. Then, 1st Lieutenant Micah Chapman, and 1st Lieutenant Miles Lundstrom accompanied Captain Locke at the side of the trail.

Lieutenant Chapman, then said, "According to my figures, Captain, we should be 20 miles, or so from where we are to leave Lieutenant Lundstrom's command, and turn southwest to Fort Richardson, Sir."

Captain Locke replied. "I came to that same conclusion, Lieutenant."

Lieutenant Lundstrom, then said, "I hope we get there with no more Indian trouble, Captain."

"I hope that as well, Lieutenant." Captain Locke replied. "It would be nice to travel unburdened by another Indian attack."

2nd Lieutenant Joe Boelinger come alongside Jamie asking, "Mind if I ride with you, Jamie?"

Jamie replied, "No, I don't mind, Joe. Glad for the company."

Joe, then said, "I didn't have the chance to say that you have inspired the men of this command. I am proud to know you, and proud to serve with you."

"Thanks, Joe." Jamie answered. "But I just did what you would've done were you in my place to save what was left of Captain Dobbs command. It was a difficult road, but we made it."

There was silence between them for a few seconds.

Then, Joe said, "I'd like to think I would've had the guts, and the will to do what you did, Jamie. I'm just not sure I would've."

Jamie said, "Aww, I'm sure you would've done the same thing I did. I'm sure of that."

Scoffing, Joe replied, "You're just bein' kind for the sake of friendship."

Jamie turned to Joe saying, "You doubtin' my word, Joe?"

Joe, then chuckled as he looked away from Jamie saying, "No, I'm just doubtin' myself. I imagine that what you did was the most arduous, and demandin' undertakin' I've ever heard of."

Jamie replied, "Well, if the truth be told, I had my moments."

Just then, 2nd Lieutenant, Flint Conyers came alongside Jamie, which left Jamie riding between the two of them.

Flint, then said, "How's your head, Lieutenant? Still have cobwebs from havin' your bell rung with that war club?"

Jamie answered with a smile, saying, "Gettin' better every day, Lieutenant. Thanks for askin'."

Soon they passed Captain Locke, 1st Lieutenant Chapman, and 1st Lieutenant Lundstrom.

Flint, then said, "I'd like to be a fly buzzin' 'round those three just to know what they're talkin' 'bout."

Joe snapped, "Not me. The less I know the better I like it. Saves me from havin' to tell a lie."

Jamie, then said, "I believe we'll know what was said when the time comes, Lieutenant, if it's in the best in'trest of his command. Who knows, they could a been talkin 'bout the weather."

Flint looked at Jamie perplexed, then said, "Nothin' rattles your brain, does it, Lieutenant? Nothin' seems to filter in on the straight skinny of things, does it?"

Jamie looked at 2nd Lieutenant Flint Conyers and his rude remarks, then replied, "Why worry 'bout things you have no control over, Lieutenant? It's goin' to happen whether we worried 'bout it or not."

Flint, then said, "We can at least be ready for what happens."

Jamie replied, "Is a man really ready for what is 'bout to happen? Seriously? I say a man is never really ready for what fate throws at him. He may think he is, but he isn't. Not really."

Chapter Four

Questions

Flint, then said, "So, what you're sayin' is, no matter how prepared a man thinks he is, he can never be fully prepared?"

Jamie answered, "That's all I'm sayin'."

Flint looked at Jamie with skepticism, then shook his head slightly saying, "That's enough."

Then, Flint reined his horse away from Jamie and 2nd Lieutenant Joe Boelinger. He inserted himself to ride between two wagons of the dead.

Joe remarked, "He's a hard man to figure out."

Jamie chuckled then said, "Not really. He has the mistaken belief that the world revolves 'round him, and one day he will realize it doesn't, much too late I'm afraid."

Joe chuckled, then said. "Won't that be a rude awakenin'?"

Jamie turned to Joe saying, "Downright offensive."

With that said, both men laughed, jostled their heads as they rode on. Near twenty miles later a couple of riders came into view of the column. One rider was said to be scout Ned Grayson. The other rider was unknown, but he was dresses in a blue cavalry uniform. As Ned Grayson and the unknown rider closed the distance between them and the column, Captain Locke called a halt. Then, the two men reined their horses in front of Captain Locke, and sat on dancing horses.

Captain Locke shouted, "Steady that mount, Grayson and give a report!"

It took a second, or two to calm his horse, he then said, "This trooper is from Fort Arbuckle. This is trooper Nelson Pitt, Captain."

Captain Locke replied, "Fort Arbuckle? You're way out of your sector are you not Private? Who's your company commander?"

Excited, and talking fast, the trooper Pitt replied, "My troop commander is Captain Silas Udall, Sir, and we was…"

Captain Locke quieted the trooper down, then asked quietly, "Where is your troop now, Private?"

Trooper Pitt replied, "Not too far from here, Captain. Southwest of our position, Sir."

"Is your troop being attacked, Private?" Captain Locke asked.

Trooper Pitt answered, "Oh, yes, Sir. The Comanche have the troop pinned down on a rocky outcrop, and they're firing down on the troop from a high rocky plateau. There is a canyon below the troop, but the Indians have snipers inside the canyon, Sir. We're ducks in a shootin' gallery, Captain."

Captain Locke then asked, "Well, then, how is it you made it out, Trooper Pitt?"

Recoiling from that question, Nelson answered shyly, "Sir, it took the lives of two of my friends for me to make it out in order to find help, and we need that help now, Captain."

Captain Locke said, "My apologies, Private for that last remark. I'll give you all the help I can."

A renewed vigor came over Trooper Pitt's countenance as he said, "Thank you, Sir."

Captain Locke turned his horse to the column, and started yelling orders to the men of his command to help rescue the command of Captain Silas Udall from Fort Arbuckle, Texas.

Captain Locke yelled out, "In my absence, Lieutenant Chapman, you have the column."

Lieutenant Chapman replied, "Yes, Sir."

Captain Locke added, "2nd Lieutenant Boelinger will remain with the column, while 2nd Lieutenant Conyers rides with me!"

2nd Lieutenant Conyers grimaced, but said, "Yes, Sir."

Captain Locke also said, "Lieutenant Lundstrom, you will be my second in command in this rescue effort!"

Lieutenant Lundstrom said, "Yes, Sir."

Captain Locke, then said, "And now every other man follow me, and Trooper Pitt, to his beleaguered troop against the Comanche." He turned his horse to the front, then shouted, "Let's move out, Private!"

Trooper Pitt kicked his horse in the flanks and took off at near gallop, followed by Ned Grayson and Captain Locke with half of his command. Their mission? To help rescue the command of Captain Silas Udall out of Fort Arbuckle, Texas, from being annihilated by the Comanche.

They traveled close to fifteen miles to the southwest, then trooper Pitt reined his horse to a halt. Captain Locke halted the company, then hollered out his orders. Gunfire was clearly heard less than a quarter mile away.

Captain Locke asked, "Show me where this canyon is, Trooper Pitt?"

"This way, Captain." Trooper Pitt replied.

Trooper Pitt kicked his horse in the flanks and led Captain Locke and the company in a westerly direction. They rode a half mile that curved like a horseshoe to the north. Then, Trooper Pitt came to a halt. Captain Locke raised his hand halting the company.

Captain Locke, then asked, "How many Indians in there, Pitt You know?"

"Not many I expect, Sir. Eight, maybe ten." Trooper Pitt replied. "No more than ten I'd think. That's all they'd need to keep us from using that as an escape route, Sir."

Captain Locke turned to the company saying "Company, dismount."

The men of the company dismounted, and waited for further orders. Captain Locke surveyed the entrance to the canyon from about fifty yards away. The gunfire was extremely close, and with the shift of the wind they could smell the gun powder.

Captain Locke, then said, "They won't be expecting any trouble from this side of the canyon, so, the element of surprise is on our side, Lieutenant."

Lieutenant Lundstrom replied, "Yes, Sir."

Captain Locke, then said, "Use knives only men, unless otherwise warranted." Pointing to Brett Covington, John Kellerman, and Tom Epps, the captain said, "You three stay with the horses. Corporal McQuarrie?"

Corporal, Angus McQuarrie replied, "Sir?"

The captain said, "Command this area well, Corporal."

Corporal McQuarrie replied in his Scottish brogue, "Aye, Captain."

The captain then said, "Let's move out."

As the men of the company headed into the canyon, they spread out in search of the Indians who were guarding the canyon against troopers from Fort Arbuckle who were trying to make their escape from the rocky outcrop. Captain Silas Udall, in command of that troop, or what was left of it, knew they had to escape that outcrop before there was no more troop to command. It was a long, painstaking effort to track down those Indians in the canyon, but to Captain Locke and Trooper Pitt, it was well worth the effort.

Although, when halfway through that ordeal, it was necessary for the use of firearms to dispatch those Indians who were alerted to the danger, and turned to face the troopers. Out on the outcrop, the sound of rifle fire from the canyon that was not aimed at the troop from Fort Arbuckle befuddled Private First Class, Ward Briggs, so, in a crouched position, he half crawled to 2nd Lieutenant, Mark Rollins, to alert him of the gunfire coming from the canyon.

Private First Class Ward Briggs said, "Lieutenant, there is gunfire comin' from the canyon."

2nd Lieutenant, Mark Rollins replied, "They've been shootin' at us from there for hours, Briggs. Every time one of us makes a break for it out through that canyon it turns into a costly mistake."

PFC Briggs replied, "Strangely enough, Lieutenant, they wasn't shootin' at us."

Lieutenant Rollins then asked, "What do you mean, they wasn't shootin' at us?"

PFC Briggs answered, "Like I said, Lieutenant, they wasn't shootin' at us." Turning to stare at the canyon, he then said, "There's somethin' mighty strange happenin' in that canyon, Sir."

2ⁿᵈ Lieutenant Rollins stared at the canyon a few seconds uttering, "Huh."

Then, he too, crouched and almost crawled to Captain Udall to alert him of what was happening in the canyon according to Private First Class, Ward Briggs. Amidst the gunfire with bullets zinging over their heads, and all around them. The bullets were careening, and ricocheting off the rocks. A couple of the troopers clutched their chests and fell from the impact of the bullet while a couple more troopers grabbed their legs, or their arm from being hit with ricocheting bullets.

2ⁿᵈ Lieutenant Rollins shouted over the roar of gunfire, "Captain, we have more problems I believe!"

Captain Udall fired his service revolver at an Indian. He fired his last bullet from the revolver, and he had to reload.

While he reloaded his weapon, Captain Udall said, "It's hard for me to believe we have more problems, Lieutenant." He breathed in and exhaled. "So, what is the problem?"

There is gunfire from the canyon, Sir." Lieutenant Rollins said. "But they aren't shootin at us, Captain."

Captain Udall replied, "We're losin' men left and right, Lieutenant, and you're tellin' me there is gunfire from the canyon?" When he had finished loading his weapon, he spoke in quiet reserve. He, then said, "Do you think it's a trick?"

Lieutenant Rollins replied, "I'm not sure Captain, but they're not shootin' at us."

"They're what?" Captain Udall answered confused.

Lieutenant Rollins replied, "They're not…"

Captain Udall replied, "I heard. I heard. Let find out what goes on in that canyon."

Without another word spoken, both the captain and the lieutenant, along with Private Ward Briggs, crouched and almost crawled close to the entrance to the canyon which was strewn with boulders and loose lifting sand. With their boot soles slipping on the rocks and sand, they finally came to a halt.

After a few seconds and no sound of gunfire, the captain said, "I don't hear anything, Lieutenant."

The lieutenant turned to Private Briggs who just shrugged his shoulders.

The lieutenant turned back to Captain Udall saying, "I don't understand it, Captain. I was told by Trooper Briggs there was gunfire coming from the canyon, Sir."

The captain looked at the lieutenant saying, "So, you, yourself, didn't hear the gunfire?"

The lieutenant recoiled saying, "Well, no, Sir, but…"

Trooper Briggs then said, "I heard the gunfire, Captain, but like I told the lieutenant, they wasn't shootin' at us. There's somethin' mighty strange goin' on in that canyon, Sir."

Captain Udall then said, "Well whatever it is, it will…."

Then, from out of the canyon, a voice came calling from nearby.

Captain Locke yelled out, "Hello, Captain Udall?"

All three men fell belly down on the rock at the sound of the voice with their weapons trained in the direction of where the voice came from.

Captain Udall said, "It could be a trick. Some of these Comanche can speak better English than you and I do."

PFC Briggs, then said, "Question is, what Comanche knows your name, and rank, Sir?"

Captain Udall replied, "That's a good question..."

Then, Captain Locked hollered again, "Captain Udall, I'm Captain Gary Locke from Fort Richardson. We have one of your troopers here, a Trooper Pitt, Nelson Pitt. He found us and was asking for our help. He let us know what you're up against, so we came to offer our help in any way we can, Sir. We took care of Comanche snipers in the canyon, so you can escape through the canyon, you and your men."

Excitedly, PFC Briggs said, "I knew there was somethin' goin' on in that canyon. I told you I heard shootin', Lieutenant."

Lieutenant Rollins replied happily, "You sure had that right, Trooper."

Excitedly, PFC Briggs said, "See, I told you there was…"

Captain Udall hollered, "Aww, quit you're cacklin', Briggs! Calm down."

Captain Locke then asked, "May I approach, Captain?"

Captain Udall smiled then said, "Approach, Captain."

Captain Locke left his position of cover to approach the mouth of the canyon, and the rocky outcrop in order to show Captain Udall it was no trick. When Captain Locke showed himself to Captain Udall, and Lieutenant Rollins both men shouted with delight.

Captain Udall, then yelled, "Lieutenant, let's get what's left of the troop out through the canyon. Thank God!"

Lieutenant Rollins replied, "Yes, Sir, Captain."

Over the roar of gunfire, Captain Udall yelled, "One by one, Lieutenant, let's get these men out a here and into the canyon! Hurry! Let's move!"

The men turned at the order of 2nd Lieutenant Rollins and Captain Udall to go into the canyon. A few men were hit with bullets to the arms or legs.

Captain Udall yelled, "Pick a man up, and move into the canyon! Quickly now!"

As the men moved as quickly as they could, the rifle fire continued. While bullets sprayed all around them, and arrows bounced off the rocks and boulders, the men under the command of Captain Silas Udall scrambled for the mouth of the canyon as fast as they could. Each man was picking up a wounded man as they tried for the canyon and safety from the onslaught of the Comanche. As the men raced for the canyon, they kept firing at the Indians on the high rocky plateau.

The men of the detachment commanded by Captain Locke raced forward to provide cover fire for the men racing for the mouth of the canyon, but Captain Locke prevented that from happening. When the last trooper of

Captain Udall's command was safely into the canyon, there came a sudden roar of relief from the men of his command. When the two captains finally met each other, they smiled, and shook each other's hand vigorously.

Captain Udall, then said, "I am in your debt, Captain."

Captain Locked replied, "Not me, Captain. You owe a debt of gratitude to Private, Ward Briggs, Sir. If not for him we would not be here."

Captain Udall, then said, "The private is now a corporal. It took a great deal of courage to do what he did, and he must be rewarded for his bravery."

Captain Locke replied, "He'll be happy to hear that, Captain. Now, let's take care of your wounded."

Captain Udall said, "Thank you, Sir. I appreciate that."

As the wounded was being treated as best they could be, Captain Locke inquired about his 1st lieutenant.

Captain Udall answered, "He's laying over by that big boulder with his face half gone. He never knew what hit him. 1st Lieutenant, Cole Trenton died a tragic death, as well as, most of my men."

Captain Locke then asked, "That's tough. Just where are your horses, Captain? Without them, you're in for a long walk."

Captain Udall replied, "They scattered at the outset of the attack. Where we are now is not where we were attacked. It's just happened to be where they herded us into… like cattle."

Captain Locke said, "Well, there's no need to guess where your mounts are."

Captain Udall sighed then said, "No, there's no need. The Comanche obviously have them."

There was silence between them as Captain Udall wearily leaned against a large boulder.

Captain Locke said, "You look all done in, Captain." Handing Captain Udall a canteen, he added, "Here have some water. It's good for what ails you." He smiled.

Captain Udall chuckled then said, "I feel worse than I look, Captain." He turned away from Captain Locke saying, "Lieutenant Rollins? Casualty report, Lieutenant!"

Standing nearby, Lieutenant Rollins replied, "Yes, Sir."

With that said, the captain removed the cork in the canteen and took a healthy swallow of water.

As he handed the canteen back to Captain Locke, Captain Udall said, "Thanks, Captain. I feel much better now."

Slim replied, "Well, wherever they are, I hope there was a good reason for them to leave with no word of any kind."

Mike said, "I can't believe they were scared off, do you?"

"They're not that kind of men." Ross answered. "That kind don't scare easy."

Slim then said, "Well, I'm tired of tryin' to second guess their move, and figure out why they left." He turned to the house saying, "I have more important things to worry 'bout."

Ross replied, "You most certainly do."

Mike then said, "And, were I you, I'd get to it, and quick."

Jenny asked, "So, I take it no one wants a cup a coffee then?"

Before anyone could answer, Jenny teared up, cried out, "Oh Danny!", and went running with tear filled eyes towards the house.

Slim lowered his head a little disheartened. He felt his spirit sink a little. He also felt the energy drain from his body like it flowed through a sieve. He, then raised his head to look towards the house as Jenny disappeared through the doorway as she entered the house, and the door closed.

Slim then said, "I see your meanin'." His chest rose and fell as he breathed deep and exhaled. He then said, "I best be goin'. Thanks for comin' to Dad's funeral. It, well, it means a lot." He turned and walked towards the house with heavy footfalls, then stopped, turned back to his friends.

Slim then said, "And, Mike, I'm glad to see you're feelin' better."

He paused as he tried his best to smile, but he knew he failed miserably in that effort.

Slim finally said, "Thank you, gentlemen." He, then turned, and walked towards the house with those same heavy footfalls.

His legs felt heavy and awfully sluggish. As he stepped into the foyer of his home, he heard the sobbing of his sister, Jennifer, and his mother, Mae. He stopped in his tracks. There was a lump in his throat that did not allow him to swallow. The door closed behind him and latched. His chest rose and fell as he took a deep breath and exhaled. He stood there barely able to collect his wits about himself. Slim struggled to keep from tearing up, so, he removed his hat, then placed it on the coat rack in the foyer. He turned to enter the living room, but the sound of his mother and his sister sobbing, and wailing in grief had finally taken its toll. He hung his head as tears welled up in his eyes to roll down his cheeks. He emitted no sound of grief, just tears, as he stood there. His chest heaving in anguish and loss. His knees began to buckle, so he sat down in the only chair in the foyer. He sat bent over as he wept with his head in his hands. His mental capacity to deal with the situation seemed to evaporate. He and his family has suffered a great loss. First, his brother, Randy, who was struck down by a sniper's bullet. Bullet? His head rose in remembrance of that hexagon bullet, and the remembrance of that bullet, caused him to sit straight up. His eyes began to sweep back and forth across the room. Bullet? How could he ever forget the Hexagon .451 caliber, single shot, muzzle loader sniper rifle hexagon bullet, and yet, he had. Realizing that all this time, that bullet was only mentioned, or even thought of, was at least four times, and now, today. Although his father, Richard, had not fallen from a sniper's bullet, but from a heart attack, that did not negate the fact that his family has been under attack from a man called, Devlin Wade. Whoever uses a hexagon .451 caliber sniper rifle is in Slim's rifle's crosshairs, and this time, the picture of that bullet is stuck in his mind's eye, and foremost in his thoughts. Slim has resolved to kill the man who uses that weapon by the most extreme torture, and penalty of death possible, and when he stops chasing that man is when that man is dead, or he himself is dead.

Matt, Victor, and Ross went to the corral where their horses was tethered. The men untethered them and mounted in order to leave the Homestead, Mike saddles his horse. The other three men waited for him to do so. Mike was definitely feeling better, but it was a little painful, to some extent, for him to saddle his horse after many days of nonuse.

Matt, then asked, "You okay, Mike?"

"Yeah, I'm okay. Just a little stiff, I reckon. It's been a while." He chuckled then added, "I must admit I'm still a little sore, but I'll work it out."

When Mike finally saddled his horse, he climbed aboard, then the four men rode away from the courtyard of the Homestead. Meanwhile, inside the house, Slim walked into the living room. There he found his sister, Jenny, and his mother, Mae, wiping tears from their eyes with a soft cloth.

Amidst the sniffling, and clearing their throat, Slim asked if they would like a glass of brandy, to which, 'no thank you', was their reply.

Slim, then said, "I hope you don't mind if I do. I sure could use it."

There came no reply. Slim poured himself two fingers of brandy.

Mae looked at her son, then said, "You've been…"

Slim butted in saying, "Yes, yes I have. I love my father, and miss him terribly. It is well within my right to show my grief at such a time as this."

Jenny replied, "It's not that you don't have the right, Danny. It's just that we never thought you'd ever show your grief. You have been the rock we needed up to and through Dad's funeral."

"Contrary to popular belief, Jenny, I am not heartless, as you know, nor am I made of stone."

He, then quickly downed his brandy, then poured another two fingers of the warm liquid.

He turned to Jenny and his mother, Mae saying, "I do have feelings, and I am allowed to display them every now and then, especially at a time of loss."

Mae, then said, "Of course you do, Danny." As she wiped her eyes she went on. "There's no harm in a man showing his grief at the loss of a loved one. It doesn't prove he's weak, and even if it did seem like it, it doesn't mean he's weak, it proves he's only human."

"I know Mother, but…"

"But, my left foot." Mae replied. "You're no weakling. You're a Siringo, and I'll not have my husband's family name be run through the mud simply by hurt feelings. No, by God, I'll not stand for any of it!"

At that said, she, again, broke down in tears. Jenny rushed to her side. As Jenny put her arm around her mother's shoulder to comfort her, she looked up at Slim with tear filled eyes.

Jenny then said, "We've had enough, Danny."

With a steadfast look on his face, and a persistent look in his eyes, he replied, "Yes, we have." As he rushed to where his gun belt was, he said, "Yes, we have had enough."

Very much concerned, Jenny asked, "What are you plannin' on doin', Danny?"

At first, Slim didn't answer as he strapped his gun belt around his waist. He took out his .45 caliber Colt revolver from its holster to check the loads. All but one round in the cylinder, He was careful to see that the hammer rested on the empty chamber as to not go off by accident. He holstered his gun, then turned to Jenny and his mother.

Mae, with concerned worry, then asked, "What *are* you goin' to do, Danny?"

"I believe it's time me and Devlin Wade had a heart to heart talk."

Jenny jumped to her feet saying, "Are you crazy? He has his gunmen protecting him, Danny. You'll not leave Comanche, but in a pine box."

Mae began to weep again, then softly said, "Today of all days, this has to happen."

Jenny looked at Slim with confusion, and unbelief. Without her saying a word, Slim got the unsaid message from Jenny. His father was just buried, and he was going to try his luck against Wade's gunmen before he got to Wade himself in a possible gunfight in the town of Comanche. He must be crazy. He slowly unstrapped his gun belt.

As he put his gun belt back where it was, he said, "There will be another day. I can wait."

He turned around to his family, then Mae said, "Thank you, Danny. I just couldn't bear the thought of losin' you too."

"I realize now, Mom, that it was a foolish thought. But, I was angry. I remember the bullet."

Jenny then said, "Of course it was. You wouldn't stand a chance against all those men of Wade's."

Mae looked a Jenny, then at Slim asking, "Bullet? What bullet?"

"No one told you, Mom?" Jenny asked.

Mae replied, "They may have, Jenny, but so many things have been said, and done here of late. I may have forgotten. I'm gettin' long in years, ya know. My memory is waning."

Slim, then said, "Doc Cousens gave me the bullet that killed Randy."

Surprised, Mae said, "He did?"

Slim answered, "Yes, he did. Doc said it was a strange lookin' bullet. He had never seen a bullet shaped that way. Sort a like a hexagonal shaped bullet."

Mae said, "Hexagon bullet? Why, I never heard of such a thing." She scoffs.

Slim sighed, then said, "I never did either, but a friend a mine bought one sometime ago. It's a beautiful weapon, but very deadly, and extremely accurate."

Mae, then asked, "And, you believe the man who uses that weapon was hired by Wade?"

"It's the only thing that fits, Mom." Slim answered. "Who would gain by killing a young boy like Randy? Answer? Devlin Wade."

Mae then said, "I don't doubt your word, Danny, but we've had trouble with Wade long before Randy was shot and killed. So, then, why kill Randy?"

"I believe that was done for two reasons." Slim replied. "One. Out of pure meanness, just because he could, and two, to prove to us that he was serious about taking our land, even if he had to get rid of each one of us, starting with Randy."

Disgusted, Mae said, "That man is a vile, and evil man. He doesn't deserve to breathe clean air."

Jenny then said, "I'm surprised he hasn't put out a wanted poster for Danny, or everyone else for that matter."

"Wanted posters he can't do. He has no legal right to print them, but, putting a price on our heads is something altogether different. It is definitely something he could do since he has just 'bout everyone in town under his control."

Jenny asked, "Isn't a wanted poster, and a price on your head the same thing, Danny? I mean, they both contain a price… alive, or dead."

"There is a definite distinction between them. One is a wanted poster, and the other Is just a circular tellin' everyone to be on the lookout for such and such, or, wanted for questioning for such and such. That's all a circular is."

Jenny replied, "They're the same thing if you ask me. Death warrants."

Mae then said, "Let's change the subject, shall we?" She shivered as if she had a chill. "I've had enough talk of death in this family."

Chapter Five

Their Last Breath

As Matt, Mike, and Victor was riding towards the cattle camp to give Slim, Jenny, and his mother, Mae, a chance to grieve as a family, the men decided to go to the cattle camp for a couple days. They rode along slow, but sure with not much conversation between them. Then, to their surprise, a group of riders came riding along the road. Six men on horseback.

As the men stared at the six men riding the road, Mike said, "Is that who I think it is?"

Matt then said, "That's who it is alright, but who do they have with them?"

Creel, riding alongside Walt asked, "You know those fellas, do ya?"

"Yes, I do." Walt replied.

When they came within feet of each other, they halted in the middle of the road.

Matt then asked, "Where in the world have you been?"

Walt asked, "How's Slim?"

Victor replied, "We just came from there. He buried his dad today. There wasn't a lot of people there, but there was enough to let you know he was well thought of."

Walt replied, "I'm sorry we missed that. How's he standin' up?"

Mike answered, "Better than we thought he would. So, who is it you have with you Walt?"

Walt replied, "These are friends of ours. There should be more comin'. I hope they get here perty soon. Anyways, the man next t me is called Creel, then there's Thaddeus Doucet, and Jonas Eberly. They've come to help get rid of Devlin Wade anyway they can."

Matt said, "Well, now, that's in'trestin'. I've heard of you Creel, and from what I hear, well... it might prove very in'trestin to see what happens.

Creel then said, "Well, since you know who we are, who are you?"

Walt replied, "Creel, this is Sheriff Matt Tucker of Stephen's County based out of Comanche. The other two are Mike Eagan, and Victor Corman. They're both wranglers for the Homestead Brand."

Creel said, "Sheriff, huh? I've heard of you. They say you're dead."

Matt replied, "If it wasn't for Walt, Fletcher, and Will here, I would be. I owe my life to them, strange as it may seem to you."

Curiously, Walt, then asked, "It seems you two know each other, other than in name only."

Matt replied, "I have. I've chased him enough times for one crime to another, and I never came close. Now, here you are."

Creel answered, "I'm here of my own free will, Sheriff, but if there's to be any trouble between me and you, let it start here and now."

Matt replied, "I respect that Creel. Your friends are of the same persuasion. Criminals, each, and everyone, but since you and your friends have come to help get rid of Devlin Wade, I suppose what stands between us can wait until that showdown is over."

Then, Thaddeus Doucet replied, "That's kind of you, Monsieur Sheriff. How noble your attitude towards Monsieur Creel."

"There's nothing noble 'bout it." Matt answered. "Remember, Monsieur Doucet, you are also a part of that awareness."

"Ah, Monsieur, I am surprised you have heard of me, and yet, I am quite delighted to know you *have* heard of me. I was becoming very much disappointed that with all of my exploits, and my most daring escapes, I was not known for none of them."

Walt then said, "How 'bout we stop reminiscing, and get on with the matter at hand."

Creel replied, "Gladly, if the sheriff will."

Thaddeus said, "Yes, the sheriff seems to have a chip on his shoulder."

"I'll gladly let the matter drop until a later time." Matt answered.

Walt, then asked, "So, where were you goin'? The Homestead is behind you."

Mike then said, "Yes, we know. We were on our way to the cattle camp to let Slim and his family be alone, and grieve as a family without any interruption."

Creel, then asked, "So, what do we do, Walt? Go bustin' in on their family grief to say, we're here? Guaranteed it will get their attention no doubt."

"No." Walt answered. "We'll wait. Then, tomorrow, we will all go to the Homestead, and let Slim know he isn't in this fight alone, and convey our condolences in losing his father."

As Flynn McDonagh, Seamus O'Neil, and Clancy Burrows left the town of Waco, Texas, they were unknowingly being followed by Brass Tacks, and a number of his men in an effort to take back the weapons that he sold to the Irishmen at Rose Glen, Texas. Since then, he had a change of mind due to the persistent wind which the Mexicans called, 'Derechos', blew across the land, setting up a shooting war between the northern, and southern states over slavery, and the southern states... claiming states' rights. He realized those guns would garner a much greater profit to the highest bidder, North, or South, if a shooting war did occur. What did he care about a far off place called, Ireland, and their fight for freedom from the British? The only thing he wanted was to have those guns back, and he would do anything to make that happen, even killing those Irishmen. Brass Tacks knew they were headed for the walnut grove northwest of town a mile, or two, but why? That he didn't know. It could be it was where they were hiding the wagon of weapons because the wagon wasn't in the barn called, Etsy. They rode hard to get to the walnut grove and take back the weapons either by hook, or by crook. As they entered the walnut grove, Flynn, Seamus, and Clancy saw the wagon at the other end of the grove as it was before, albeit, they didn't see Brass Tacks and his men following them. Tim and Kevin didn't see them at the time either. But, as the three came closer and closer riding through the row of walnut trees, Tim and Kevin noticed movement behind them. They then saw who it was coming on fast behind them. Tim and Kevin scurried to get the tarpaulin off of a crate of rifles, and some ammunition for each rifle. Flynn noticed at a distance what Tim and Kevin was up to, so, he turned his head to look back. It was then when he saw Brass Tacks and his men riding hard towards them, and quickly gaining ground.

When they came to the wagon of weapons, each man hurriedly dismounted while each man was tossed a rifle and ammunition. They spooked their horses, then quickly ran to other side of the wagon, and watched as Brass Tacks and his men came roaring in with gunfire. Bullets began to chip away at the wagon or whizzed by their heads as Brass Tacks and his men fired at the Irishmen. Then, the Irishmen fired back in a volley of fire and smoke. A couple of Brass Tacks' men fell from their horses to lay in the leaves and sediment of the walnut grove. Brass Tacks shouted his orders, then his men dismounted, and they ran for cover behind the trees. The gun battle erupted through the grove, and gun smoke filled the air. A couple of Brass Tacks' men ran to trees which was closer to the wagon, but were shot down.

They lay dead in the leaves and sediment of the walnut grove. Brass Tacks realized he was losing men he couldn't afford to lose. The gun battle slowed down to almost no firing whatsoever.

Brass Tacks yelled out, "McDonagh, you and those with you can leave the wagon of weapons, and no harm will come to you! Did you hear that Men!? No harm to them if they leave! You have horses, McDonagh, so, use them to leave! All I want are those weapons. What do you say!?"

Flynn then said, "How 'bout you and your men mounting up, and leaving us alone!?"

"We paid dearly for those weapons, McDonagh." Brass Tacks replied. "The price was friends of mine!"

Sean then yelled out, "We paid good money to you for these guns, you lout! Our countrymen needs these guns, and I'll not be handin' them over to the likes of you, Brassy Lad. Heh, heh, heh!"

Brass Tacks then asked, "Are those guns worth dyin' for!?"

Flynn replied, "You should ask those who died tryin' to get them back!"

With genuine anger, Brass Tacks hollered, "I'll feed your eyes to the wolves. You can count on that, McDonagh!"

Flynn chuckled saying, "I believe you told me that before, but I'm still here, Lane!"

Rattled, Brass Tacks yelled out, "Only my friends call me that, and no one else. You're no friend of mine, Irishman!"

Flynn then said, "And now, your enemies will call you, Lane. Ha, ha, ha, ha. I'll share your real name wherever I go!"

Brass Tacks replied, "You won't live that long. McDonagh!"

Flynn yelled back, "You have yet to convince me of that!"

Screaming, Brass Tacks yelled, "I want those guns!"

Kevin then yelled, "Bugger off, Lane, or you will die here in this walnut grove!"

Silence fell on the grove for a span of about fifteen minutes. Lane flip flopped from one side of the tree to the other, angry as a wet hen. Then suddenly, and without warning, gunfire erupted. Splinters of wood flew in every direction as bullets from Brass Tacks and his men ripped into the weapons wagon in search of the men on the other side. Their gunfire was then answered from the five Irishmen behind the wagon. Both sides missing each other, but barely doing so. A man jumped from the cover of a walnut tree, firing his weapon at the Irishmen as he went, in order to find better cover by a pile of walnut cut logs that was closer to the wagon, but he was shot down before he could get there.

Flynn, then asked, "How many were there at the start of this fight?"

Tim replied, "Seven, I think, not counting Brass Tacks."

Flynn said, "If I counted right, Lads, there is only Lane, and one other man left to contend with."

Seamus then said, "You've always been able to count, and count good too."

Clancy said, "Then, we have him out numbered."

Kevin replied, "I wouldn't step out there for all the guns in America."

Clancy then said, "Then, we just wait him out?"

Flynn replied, "We can't. You forget you have a boat to catch, and we need to get these guns to Matagorda on the coast before the boat sails."

Clancy then said, "Well, we wouldn't want that to happen now, would we!?"

Sean said, "For the love of Mike, no, we wouldn't!"

Then, Brass Tacks yelled out, "Mark!? You good on ammunition!?"

Mark Jernigan yelled back, "I've got plenty, Lane!"

"How 'bout you, Ed!?" Brass Tacks hollered. "Ed!?" Getting no answer, he then yelled, "How 'bout you, Ben!?" Still, no answer. "Jim!?" No reply. "Henry!?" No reply. "Frank!?" No reply. A little discouraged, he yelled, "Rex, you still here!?"

Rex Tibbs hollered back, "I'm still here, Lane! Same as Mark! I have plenty!"

Grinning like a bird fed cat, Lane replied, "That's good to know!"

He leaned his back against the walnut tree as he reloaded his revolver.

He then turned to the weapons wagon yelling out, "We're comin for those guns, you scum!"

Tim hollered, "You'll die tryin', Lane!"

Brass Tacks yelled back, "That remains to be seen, Irishman, but I wouldn't bet on it! You'd lose, heh, heh, heh!"

Just then, Clancy dropped to the ground and lay behind the front wheel of the wagon. Then the rest spread out along the wagon. They grabbed handfuls of ammunition as they went, filled their pockets, and reloaded their weapons. As the wind blew the gun smoke from the grove, gunfire exploded again. Bullets were whizzing past their heads and began chipping away the wood on the wagon.

All it would take is one perfectly aimed bullet to hit the ammunition box, and the whole shebang would go up like a roman candle, killing, or wounding anyone standing near it. Gun smoke, again, filled the air. Gunfire echoed through the grove and beyond.

Brass Tacks hollered, "You're goin' to die, McDonagh, and your friends!"

Tim told Clancy, "You better get out from under the wagon, Lad. Find a cover quite away from the wagon."

Clancy yelled back, "Why? I have a good field of fire."

Tim replied, "You're also in a good spot to get blown to smithereens, as we all are. We need to get away from the wagon."
Clancy began to crawl out backwards from under the wagon.

Flynn, then asked, "Why do we need to get away from the wagon? Tis great protection."

"Aye, it would be, but all it would take is one ill-placed bullet to hit the ammunition box, and it goes up like a roman candle, and us with it."

Clancy shouted, "Jumpin' Jehosephat! Now you tell us!"

Tim then said, "You'd better leg it, Lads. Quickly now."

Each man scrambled for cover away from the wagon as the wagon was peppered with bullets. Bullets spit up dirt, leaves, and sediment, and went whizzing past the men as they dashed for cover away from the wagon.

Brass Tacks hollered, "They're runnin'! Let's get to those guns!"

All three men rushed from their cover, shooting as they ran. Before the Irishmen found cover, they fired as they ran. Brass Tacks was running in the row of the walnut grove firing his weapon, when a bullet cut into his stomach. His face exploded in surprise as his mouth went ajar. He grabbed his middle. He staggered a little as he turned to run, but he fell over on his face… dead. The two men who were left, Mark Jernigan, and Rex Tibbs, ran up the row of the walnut grove towards the wagon, firing their guns as they ran. Mark Jernigan was hit in the chest, and from the impact of the bullet, he fell backwards into the leaves, and sediment. Rex Tibbs seen what happened to his friend, Mark Jernigan, he came to a standstill beside a walnut tree. As he looked around the tree to fire, a bullet struck him in the head. His head flew backwards from the impact.

He collapsed at the tree down onto his knees in the leaves, and in the sediment of the walnut grove, his body leaning against the tree…dead. Believing the threat was over, they came from their hiding places. It was just a second, or two when another shot rang out. The bullet went whizzing past Clancy's head. Clancy quickly turned to see where the bullet hit. It splattered into a walnut tree, sending tree bark and tiny wood splinters into the air. As the Irishmen, again, sprinted for cover, shock and surprise showed on their faces.

Flynn hollered, "I thought we got rid of everyone a them Brass Tacks' men."

Clancy replied, "I thought so too. That nearly took my head off."

Tim then asked, "Well, who is shootin' at us then?"

Kevin asked, "Anyone know where that shot come from?"

George Craddock's voice echoed through the walnut grove, "You didn't think we forgot 'bout you, did you, Clancy!?"

Clancy replied, "I know that voice. But it couldn't be. He's in jail, or was."

Tim, then asked, "Well, just who is it, Lad?"

Flynn answered, "He's that fella who tried to get past you and have a look in the wagon."

"That's him alright." Clancy replied.

Seamus then said, "He drew a gun on you, but the sheriff come along and arrested him."

"That's true. He was also tossed in jail, so, how did he get out?"

Flynn answered, "Who knows?"

Clancy yelled out, "George!? George Craddock!? You hear me, George!?"

George let out with a wild cackle, then said, "Yeah, I hear ya, Clancy! What do

you want!?"

Clancy replied, "You bring your friends with you!?"

First, Clay Bricker hollered, "Clay Bricker here, Clancy!"

Then, Arron Short hollered, "I'm here too. The name's, Arron Short!"

Then, Jake Blanchard hollered, "Don't forget me, Clancy! Jake Blanchard here!"

Charley Hornaday hollered, "Charley Hornaday, Clancy! I'm here to take revenge!"

Flynn hollered, "What did he ever do to you!?"

Charley hollered back, 'When you do to one, you do to all! We spent time in jail, and now, we need to get compensation for doin' so!"

Flynn asked, "Just how did you get out a jail!? You break out!?"

"It doesn't matter how we got out!" George replied. "The thing is, we are out, and we've come lookin' for Clancy!"

Flynn asked, "And, why is that?"

"We have unfinished business, he and I." George answered.

Seamus, then hollered, "You'll have to go over us first, Mister!"

George let go with another wild cackle, then said, "I see no problem in that! We left something unsettled between us."

Clancy asked, "And what would that be, Craddock!? You shootin' me down and

me with no weapon to defend myself!?"

"You have one now, so, use it!" George shouted back. "But either way I'm goin' to kill you, Clancy, and I'll kill anyone who gets in my way!"

Seamus then said, "As I said, Mister, you'll have to come through us to get to hm."

George gave a wild cackle, then said, "I 'spect to reckon we're done jabber jawin', then!?"

With that said, he cocked his hand gun and fired it at Clancy, who took cover behind the walnut tree. The bullet struck the tree with a thud, and buried itself deep in the tree removing some of the tree bark, but nothing else.

Then, the rest of the men with him began to fire at the Irishmen.

The gun battle lasted but a few minutes, then a bullet was fired from behind Craddock near the entrance of the walnut grove. George quickly turned to the sound of the rifle shot, and saw three men take cover behind walnut trees at the entrance of the grove. Confused and surprised, he slid down the tree to kneel on one knee on the ground. His friends who came with him saw that they were in a crossfire. The Irishmen had stopped their shooting and looked on, also in confusion and surprise. George turned to look at Clancy, then turned back to the three men who entered the walnut grove.

After a few seconds, George hollered, "Who are you, Mister!?"
Then, the voice echoed through the grove, "A. K. Masters, sheriff of Waco Texas,

and deputies at your service, Craddock!"
"Why'd you follow me, Sheriff!?"

"Why!?"

George let out a wild cackle, then said, "I asked first!"

Sheriff Masters then said, "You and your friends have spent time in my jail recently for exactly what you're doin', but now, you're lookin' at a murder charge! You'll hang for it! Don't make me kill you, Son, and you know I'll do 'er too! So, all a ya, drop your guns, and come out with your hands up, you're all under arrest!"

George hollered, "How could that be, Sheriff!? We haven't done anything to be arrested for!"

"Only because we followed you and tried to stop you!" Sheriff Masters answered. "Now, the charge is attempted murder instead of murder since you tried to shoot Mister Burrows!"

Goerge, then cackled wildly saying, "I'm through talkin', Sheriff!"

Sheriff Masters hollered, "Don't do it, Son! You die here and now!"

With a wild cackle, George turned back to Clancy, then he and those with him, started shooting at Clancy and the Irishmen, which the Irishmen felt obliged to return gunfire. Then, sheriff A.K. Masters and his deputies opened up on George and his friends. George was hit three times in the body, and once in the right arm causing him to drop his gun. Blood began to appear at the edges of his mouth, and then he began to cough up blood. His friends were also wounded, but they were able to walk out of the grove, except for Aaron Short, and Jake Blanchard who lay dead in the leaves and the sediment of the walnut grove. Sheriff Masters walked up to George with his gun cocked and ready.

The sheriff looked down on George and shook his head.

Sheriff Masters sighed heavily, then said, "This could've turned out so different, if you would've just listened to me."

George leaned against the tree. He tried to raise his head to look at Sheriff Masters, but he found he couldn't.

As blood ran down his chin, George replied, "My choice, Sheriff." he coughed. "I would've died in prison, one way, or the other." He coughed. "Prison doesn't offer much room… for a… a man to spit."

George breathed his last as he knelt on one knee, leaning against the tree.

As Sheriff Masters looked around the walnut grove, he shook his head saying, "Looks like a damn battlefield. Bodies everywhere."

Sheriff deputies, Jim Wagner, and Howard Dunsberry, held their guns on Charley Hornaday, and Clay Bricker, both wounded, as they walked out of the walnut grove to their horses, then off to jail. The Irishmen came running up to Sheriff Masters as they looked down at the bodies of Brass Tacks men and of Brass Tacks himself.

Flynn then asked, "Have you heard of a man they call Brass Tacks, Sheriff?"

"Who hasn't?" The sheriff relied. "I'd love to get my hands on that man. I'd be set for life."

Flynn then said, "Follow me."

They walked to a tree a little closer to the wagon where Brass Tacks was sitting on the ground, leaning against a tree… dead.

Sheriff Masters asked, "Who is he?"

Flynn pointed to Brass Tacks saying, "Him? That my good man is, Lane Talbot."

"Lane Talbot?" The sheriff said. "I ain't never heard a him."

"Lane Talbot is his real name, Sheriff, but he went by the monicker, Brass Tacks."

"Brass Tacks?" The sheriff asked in surprise. "Are you sure that man is Brass Tacks?"

Flynn answered, "Quite sure, Sheriff. We had an off and on relationship, you might say. He also tried to kill us, well actually me, but, as you can see, we didn't let him."

"Yes, I see." The sheriff replied. "No, I don't see. Why did he want to kill you?"

Flynn answered, "Tis a long story, Sheriff, but the short of it is the same reason that George Craddock wanted to kill Clancy. We ran into him and his bunch in a place called Rose Glen, and the same thing occurred, but his anger was with me. I guess he didn't like Irishmen."

Silence between them for a few seconds as Sheriff Masters stared at the body of Brass Tacks, aka, Lane Talbot.

Then, Flynn asked, "So, what now, Sheriff, and what 'bout these bodies? You need us to stay and testify against those two men?"

The sheriff answered, "No. it isn't necessary. Me, and my deputies can testify to their attempted murder charge. We can handle things here. I must let you know, though, that there is a five thousand dollar reward for the capture of Brass Tacks as of the last wanted poster on him. No picture, just a description." He sighed then said, "I'll have the undertaker, Ben McQue, bring out a buckboard, and a couple men to pick up these bodies, and he can bury them proper… up on boot hill."

Kevin, then asked, "So, we're free to go, Sheriff?"

"I don't see why not." The sheriff answered. "You're all free to go. Like I said, we can handle things here."

Tim said, "Good. We can be on our way then."

Flynn said, "I believe I'll stick around a few days. It's been a rough few days."

Seamus, then asked, "Mind if I go with you, Flynn?"

"Not at all, Lad." Flynn replied. "I'd appreciate the company of a Darlin' Mucker."

Tim, and Kevin walked back to the wagon.

Sheriff Masters had a confused look on his face as he asked, "Do you mind tellin' me what a Darlin' Mucker is? I have a disagreeable feeling with hearin' that."

Seamus chuckled, then answered, "Ah, 'tis a render of a dear friend, Sheriff.

Mucker is the Irish word for friend."

The sheriff smiled, then replied, "I'm glad to hear you say that. You wouldn't believe what I was thinkin' a Mucker was, let alone a Darlin' Mucker."

Flynn then said, "Aye. 'Tis a different language I'm afraid."

Clancy said, "I'll catch up the horses, Flynn."

Flynn replied, "Thanks, Clancy."

As Clancy leaves to catch up the horses, Tim and Kevin go back to the wagon to inspect the damage caused by the bullets. There they found quite a few bullet holes, and some chunks of wood missing, but nothing that would hinder its use. It took a few minutes to catch up the horses, but when he had, Clancy tethered Flynn and Seamus' horses to a low hanging limb of the walnut tree.

Then, Flynn and Seamus walked back to the wagon to bid their friends a sad farewell, and a safe journey to Matagorda on the coast, while Sheriff Masters turned and followed his deputies to their horses at the entrance to the walnut grove. When the sheriff got to the edge of the grove, he stopped, turned, and surveyed the grove shaking his head. He then turned and walked away. Each man smiled as they looked into the friendly faces of their friends. They shook hands vigorously as they wished each other a long life full of happiness and love. Then Tim and Kevin climbed aboard the wagon. Then, Tim picked up the reins and slapped the reins over the backs of the draft horses. As the wagon pulled away from the walnut grove, Clancy mounted his horse and followed the wagon. Flynn and Seamus waved goodbye to their friends.

They turned to their horses, untied them from the tree limb, then mounted. They rode to the other side of the grove, then followed trail back to Waco. Deputies Dunsberry and Wagner locked their prisoners in their cells, and went for Doctor Carl Mendelson, to care for their wounds. Sheriff A.K. Masters reined in at Ben McQue's mortuary, stepped down from the saddle, and went in.

The sheriff yelled out, "Ben, you here? Hey, Ben?"

Getting no reply, he headed for the back door thinking he was cleaning the hearse, or something. When he got to the rear of the mortuary, that was exactly what Mortician Ben McQue was doing… cleaning the hearse. The rear doors of the hearse was standing opened with Ben cleaning the inside.

Chapter Six

Promises on Paper

Ben was putting up fresh, clean curtains in the widows. He stood, stooped over to sweep out the hearse when Sheriff Masters walked up.

The sheriff said, "Hello, Ben. How's business?"

Ben turned to see Sheriff Masters, then said, "Well, hello, Sheriff. What brings you by?"

The sheriff replied, "I have business for you, Ben. You and a couple men are needed at the walnut grove."

Ben then said, "I thought you said you had business for *me*? It isn't pickin' walnuts is it? I have no in'trest in it."

Sheriff Masters then said, "No, it ain't pickin' walnuts, but I do have business for you, and the business I have for you is in the walnut grove. You'll need a buckboard and a couple men to load the bodies on, and then taken to Boot Hill to be buried."

Ben looked at Sheriff Masters excitedly saying, "Bodies? Did you say… dead bodies?"

"What other kind a bodies are there, Ben? Of course they're dead."

Sounding disheartened, Ben said, "Oh." Then, went on, "How many bodies are there?"

"Six, I think. County will pay for your trouble."

"Do you want these bodies buried in a pine box, or not?"

"However, it suits you, Ben, that will be up to you. But don't you think building those boxes will take a day, or two delayin' their burial? Just a thought, but like I said, the county will pay for their undertakin'."

After arrangements were made with Ben McQue, the undertaker, and mortician, Sheriff Masters left the mortuary on his way to the sheriff's office. When he arrived at his office, he found Doc Mendelson bandaging the prisoners' wounds, Charley Hornaday, and Clay Bricker in a cell, and he found Flynn McDonagh, and Seamus O'Neil waiting.

Sheriff Masters then said, "The county will pay the bill for their medical needs, Doc. Not to worry 'bout that."

Doc Mendelson chuckled as he wrapped the bandage around Clay Bricker's right arm from a gunshot wound.

Doc said, "Sounds like free gratis again, Sheriff?"

Leaning against the doorjamb to the cells, Sheriff Masters replied,

"You sound as though you have a grudge against the county on payin' their medical bills, Doc."

"Who, me? Naw. I wouldn't think of sayin' that." Doc answered sarcastically. "It's just you can't eat promises printed on paper, especially those that were made, and then forgot. I still have a few bills that should've been paid by the county from last year. If I remember right…"

Sheriff Masters butted in saying, "Alright, Doc, alright. I get the message, but I just work for the county. I'm not in charge of payin' their bills, but if I were…"

Doc butted in saying, "Yeah, I know. I'd be getting my overdue bills paid, plus todays medical bill."

Sheriff Masters then said, "That's right, Doc. You'd get your bills paid."

Doc replied, "Were I to get paid at least once, my heart couldn't handle it. Why, I'd have a stroke, or somethin'."

Sheriff Masters then said, "You're kind a layin' it on a little thick, ain't ya, Doc?"

Doc Mendelson chuckled saying, "Could be." He slapped the arm he just wrapped with bandage saying, "That ought a hold ya."

Charley Hornaday cried out, "Hey, watch it, Doc. That hurts."

Doc replied, "Sorry. Forgot myself."

Sheriff Masters raised himself off of the doorjamb, turned and went and sat down at his desk.

The sheriff looked to Flynn and Seamus saying, "Pay him no never mind. He's just sore he hasn't been paid for his services by the county yet." He smiled, then said, "So, what can I do for you gentlemen?"

Just then, Doc Mendelson walked into the office from the cell area, saying, "Toss me the keys, and I'll lock the cell doors."

Sheriff Masters said, "They're hangin' to your right there on the wall, Doc."

Doc took the ring of keys hanging on a peg on the wall to his right, then went back into the cell area and closed, then locked the cell door. He entered the office and hung the keys back on the peg. Sheriff Masters took out pencil and paper, then wrote on the paper $2.50 owed to Doctor, Carl Mendelson of Waco, Texas, county of McLennan, county seat, Waco, Texas.

Doc asked, "What do you think you're doin'?"

Sheriff Masers replied, "I thought that would be obvious, Doc. I'm giving you a receipt for services rendered."

Doc replied, "Good. I can always put it with my other promissory notes that are gatherin' dust on my desk."

Sheriff Masters then said, "Well, if you put them in a drawer, Doc, they wouldn't be gatherin' dust."

"Cute. Real funny." Doc answered. "You should hire yourself out to a comedy tour. You'd make a buck, or two."
Sheriff Masters chuckled, then said, "Sounds like a fair deal, plus it'd be a whole lot safer."

"Humph!" Doc said. "Somehow I knew you'd find some way to make that sound like a good idea."

Doc walked over to pick up his hat from off the small table across the room.

He then walked to the door saying, "Well, I suppose I'll…"

Sheriff Masters reached out his hand with the promissory note in it saying, "Don't forget this IOU, Doc. The amount is written on it. Can't pay ya unless you have this, ya know." He smiled.

Doc scoffed then said, "Don't pay *with* one."

Doc walked over to the desk, snatched the IOU from the sheriff's hand, went to the door and opened it, stepped out, stopped, turned to look back at Sheriff Masters, shook his head, then, turned and left the sheriff's office, closing the door behind him as he walked on down the boardwalk.

Sheriff Masters chuckled, then said, "He's one of a kind, Doc is. This town would be lost without him, and in a real bad hurt."

Seamus then said, "He does seem to be reasonable sort, doesn't he?

Turning his attention to Flynn and Seamus, he asked, "Did I ask what I could do for you?"

Seamus replied, "I believe you asked, 'just what can I do for you, gentlemen'?, is the way it went, Sheriff."

Sheriff Masters said, "Thanks for clarifyin' that….?"

"The name's, Seamus O'Neil constable. Seamus O'Neil."

"Well, Mister O'Neil, how can I help you two?"

Flynn replied, "We just came to thank you for helpin' us out of a wee bit of trouble we were in back in that walnut grove."

Sheriff Masters replied, "Just doin' my job as sheriff."

Seamus then said, "T'was too many all at once. Tis a grand thing you done, Constable."

Flynn asked, "How long before we get that reward money, Sheriff."

"You'll get your money. It'll take a couple days though, maybe more."

Flynn replied, "That'll be fine, Sheriff. We have use for that money."

Sheriff Masters said, "Who doesn't. I wouldn't mind getting' hold a some a that money myself."

Flynn replied, "Well, now, that can be arranged."

"I like what you say…?"

"The name's, Flynn McDonagh. If truth be told, sheriff, a part of that reward money belongs to you."

Sheriff Masters looked at Flynn confused, "How do you figure that, Mister McDonagh?"

"Well, the way I see it, if it wasn't for you and your deputies, we would still be stuck in the walnut grove feedin' the worms, as you might say. So, we believe a portion of that money is yours, and your deputies."

Sheriff Masters, then asked, "Just how much do you believe that amount would be?"

Flynn looked at Seamus who just shrugged his shoulders.

Flynn answered, "Now that is a conundrum, Sheriff. There seems to be no even number to spread equally three ways."

The sheriff then said, "Ah, you forgot my deputies, Mister McDonagh."

Flynn replied, "So, I did, Sheriff. So, I did. Well, I figured that sum of money would come from your share of the reward since they are your deputies under your charge, as it were."

The sheriff then said, "So, in other words, my share would equal three shares. Is that what you're sayin?"

Flynn answered, "Aye. That is what we're sayin', Sheriff."

Devlin Wade came from his office and walked into the bar area. He, then walked up to the bar and stood as if looking for something, or someone. Fred, the bartender was at the other end of the bar pouring drinks for customers at the bar. When he had finished, he walked the length of the bar to stand opposite of where Wade was standing.

In a jovial tone, Fred asked, "What can I get for ya, Boss?"

Wade found who he was looking for, Paul Stroud, and Karl Stokes, but both men had their heads down on their table out cold from too much rot gut whiskey.

Wade scoffed crankily, then turned to Fred saying, "Give me a bottle of my finest red wine, Fred."

Fred scoffed, then said, "Wine? In this heat?"

Wade didn't look at the bartender, he just grumpily said, "Fred."

"Yes, Sir." Fred turned away, then turned back saying, "And a wine glass?"

Fred instantly knew he asked a stupid question, and the expression on his face gave it away. Why didn't he just bring a wine glass, then he would've escaped the ridicule. Wade slowly turned his head to Fred with an unbelieving glare.

Seeing the look on Wade's face, Fred swallowed hard, then said, "Yes, Sir."

Fred walked on down the bar as Wade rubbed his left temple with his fingers.

He closed his eyes as he massaged his temple trying to rub away a headache. He found massaging his temple was quite soothing, even after a few seconds of massaging.

Without opening his eyes, Wade said, "I've hired morons."

It took a few minutes for Fred to come back with Wade's finest California red wine. A Maison Montagne big red blend. It reveals a delightful interplay of ripe strawberries, and freshly pressed Blackcurrants. A medium body that envelopes the senses with the vibrancy of red fruits, red berries, graceful floral notes that lingers on the tongue. It is composed of 50% Merlot, 30% Cabernet Sauvignon, and 20% Syrah. Wade was also given a hefty, long-stemmed wine glass. After putting the bottle of wine and wine glass on the bar, Fred quickly looked busy elsewhere, but he kept looking at Wade out of his peripheral vision, waiting for the inevitable ridicule. Wade noticed it, but he scoffed at it. He, then ignored it as he took up his bottle of fine wine from California, and the wineglass. He, then walked through the crowd of drunks, low-life's, criminals of all sorts, and assorted painted ladies to make a man spend more than he can afford, as he headed back to his office at the rear of the Lucky Deuce Saloon.

Captain Locke then said, "We need to get you and your men out of this canyon."

Captain Udall answered, "We'll be slowed down by all the wounded, Captain, but we'll do the best we can."

Captain Locke then said, "I'm sure you will, Captain. The Comanche have the high ground, so we must hurry as much as possible, or we'll never escape the hands of those red devils."

Captain Udall turned and began to shout orders to his men. Each man, then picked up a wounded man who had shoulder wounds, or leg wounds, or other unmentionable wounds, and they began to move towards the other end of the canyon. The men moved as quickly and as orderly as they could.

Captains Locke and Udall were ushering their men to the other end of this canyon.

Captain Locke kept saying, "Move along, men. Quickly now. Move along. Hurry. Hurry."

Captain Udall was parroting the same things Captain Locke was saying as the men moved past them. The Comanche on the rocky plateau wondered why there wasn't any return fire from the troopers on the rocky outcrop, so the chief sent a couple of scouts on foot to find out why. The scouts crept up close to the rocky outcrop just to find dead troopers, but not one wounded man, nor troopers to fight back. The scouts quickly raced back to their chief to let him know what they found.

In a huff, the chief ordered the move from the rocky plateau to the entrance to the canyon. He ordered ten braves to hurry to the other side of the canyon beyond the rocky outcrop to trap the white eyes in order to kill each and every white man for trespassing on Indian land. The braves quickly caught up their ponies, then mounted them, and raced off in a hurry to trap the white eyes inside the canyon enabling them to annihilate the white eyes. The troopers hustled as quickly as they could with the wounded, hampering their quick escape through the canyon. The chief of the Comanche war party and his braves raced from the rocky plateau to the rocky outcrop in order to follow the troopers in the canyon. The chaos of trying to outsmart the other was, well, chaotic. Hahahaha. Uh, sorry. On with the story. While the troopers were running away from the Comanche, the Comanche was hurrying to get in place to kill all the white eyes in the land of their forefathers. It had taken quite some time for the troopers to get to the other side of the canyon, what being hindered by the wounded, but they came to the entrance to the canyon. When the troopers of Captain Udall's command exited the canyon, they found horses were waiting, and four troopers on guard. Trooper after trooper exited the canyon, with the wounded being helped by the troopers. The troopers were tired and out of breath and began to sit on the ground to rest, thus relieving themselves of the weight of the wounded. The wounded were themselves in a unstable situation. As Captains Udall and Locke emerged from the canyon, they noticed the condition of the men. Captain Locke understood the men were tired, and wore out, but they had better move quickly, or they would all be dead.

Captain Locke shouted to the detachment, "Let the wounded ride. Let's get them on a horse quickly. We need to move and move fast. I think we're just a few minutes, or less, from being fired on by the Comanche trying to get ahead of us to the mouth of this canyon. Let's move, people!"

Captain Udall then said, "Let's get up and get movin', men. Let's keep them Comanche well in our hindsight."

There came a grumbling from a few of the men which was somewhat expected, so neither captains gave credence to their grumblings. Men will be men, and you can only push a man so far until he balks, and then he refuses to listen to commands of a superior officer, or to anything he deems unfavorable to his dilemma.

Even though the men grumbled, and aired their disappointments, they picked themselves up, grabbed a wounded man, and put that wounded man on a horse.

Captain Locke then said, "Let's get back to the column, Captain. I feel that if we

don't get there, and soon, we may be too late."

Captain Udall replied, "You have a column, Captain? I had no idea."

"When we're free of the Comanche, and their villainous ways, I will explain, Sir."

"It's just a comfort to know you have one, Captain." Captain Udall then said.

The wounded were put on horses, and the troopers began to jog beside the horses of the wounded. They were hoping they would get away from the danger that was ever pressing against them.

Then, Captain Locke shouted, "If the wounded man can bare it, wherever it is possible, ride double. We have a long way to go to get to the column."

Captain Udall noticed that one of the wounded men had passed out, and was leaning to the right at the point of falling out of the saddle.

Captain Udall screamed out, "Someone help that man!"

Corporal Angus McQuarrie rushed to that wounded man from a few yards away. Then, the man fell from the saddle into the arms of the corporal McQuarrie. The corporal laid the man down on the ground as the bedraggled troop halted. Searching for a heartbeat, he found none.

Captain Locke then hollered, "Corporal, how is that man?"

"This man is dead, Captain."

Captain Locke turned to Captain Udall then said, "Let's keep movin'."

Captain Udall looked at the dead body of the trooper, then said, "Move out, men."

As the men passed the body of the trooper, they stared with no emotion in their eyes.

One trooper stared at the body of the trooper as he passed by, then said, "That's Rudy! That's Rudy Bidwell, Captain!"

"I know who it is, Teague!" Captain Udall hollered back. Then, his voice softened, "Keep your intervals." He then hollered at the troop, "Keep up. All-a-ya! No lollygaggin'!"

The bedraggled detachment traveled close to seven miles without a break, stopping only when necessary, and happily with no sign of the Comanche to cause chaos and death. along as quickly as possible. Rest, when possible, then up and at 'em again. Finally, two troopers came riding up to the bedraggled troop sent from the column to find out what happened to Captain Locke and the detachment. As the two troopers rode up to the captain, Private Carl Streat, the other galloper for Captain Locke to Fort Richardson, sat on a dancing horse looking down on the bedraggled detachment. Captain Locke smiled with wonder when he saw who the two troopers were, they were Corporal Wirt Jensen, and Private Carl Streat from the column. Captain Locke looked at Captain Udall, smiled, then turned back to the two troopers sitting their horses.

Captain Locke then said, "Streat! Man am I glad to see you made it, Trooper. Did you get to Fort Richardson?"

Carl Streat replied, "I did, Sir. They'll be along directly, Sir. I was sorry to hear 'bout Hugh, I mean, Trooper McCracken, Captain. He was a good soldier, and a good friend."

"How far behind you are the reinforcements, Streat?"

"Oh, four, five hours, give or take, Sir, but they're a comin', Captain. Lickety-split."

"Lieutenant Chapman sent you I assume?"

Corporal Jensen answered, "He did, Sir. He got kind a worried 'bout what may have happened to you and the detachment. Just as I was as I was 'bout to leave, Streat here, come ridin' in. That's when he made his report to

Lieutenant Chapman, then the lieutenant ordered us to come find you, Sir."

"Well, I certainly am glad you did, Corporal. Now, you go back, and you tell Lieutenant Chapman that Captain Udall and I, plus the detachment, we'll be along directly."

Slim sat down in a chair in his living room at the Homestead, but then a few seconds later he stood and walked back to where the brandy was. He looked at the brandy bottle with a sneer of disgust, then turned from it.

His mother, Mae, said, "What's the matter, Danny? You act like a cat on a hot tin roof for some reason. So, what's the matter? What's got you so wound up?"

Slim replied, "I can't get my mind off a that hexagon bullet, Mom. I need to find out who uses that kind a weapon, and take him down like the no good coyote that he is. And when, and if I get my hands on him, I'll wring his scrawny, little neck like I would a Bantam chicken."

Jenny then said, "Well, just don't go flyin' off the handle, Danny. Don't go and do somethin' stupid that you get yourself killed."

"I won't, Jenny" Slim replied. "Trust me, I don't have my head on sideways. I'm thinkin' straight." He begins to walk back and forth in the living room. "It just gets my dander up to know that that man is somewhere in town, and I can't go in there without getting' myself shot. Plus, I am a little upset that Walt, Fletcher and Will just up and leaves without a single word 'bout it, or a given reason for it."

Mae then said, "I know you have your heart set on somethin', Son, but please be careful. Think before you act. Like I said, I've had enough talk of death in this house. I don't want to hear no more of it."

"I will take great pleasure in puttin' the man who uses that gun in his grave just like he did, Randy. I'll see that man dead if it's the last thing I ever do."

Mae then said, "Well, I believe that man, whoever he is, can wait till later. Right now, though, you need to grieve at your father's passing, and I will grieve my husband's. I figure at least a day of mournin' for both is what is needed, Danny."

Slim replied, "You're right, Mom, as usual. I'll give it the rest of the day, then come mornin'…."

Jenny then said, "Come mornin'? Then what, Danny? You haven't got a clue how to do that, do ya, except, maybe, get yourself killed."

"I'm not goin' to do anything halfcocked, Jenny." Slim replied. "I'll be as careful as I can, and you know that, but I must find out who uses that rifle, and put him down if I can. I've let it slip my mind too many times. Never again. I swear."

Jenny said, "I believe it's goin' to be a nice, quiet day around here, so with that in mind, I think I'll bake a cake, a pie, or even cookies just to keep my mind off a things."

Mae then said, "I'll join you my dear, if only to clear my mind just to create a fondness for all the memories that will come floodin' in."

Slim replied, "I'm not a baker, nor a cook, Mom."

Mae said, "Well, then, I'll make you a pot of coffee to dilute the brandy you've been drinkin'. Clear your head. I could use a cup myself, and I know you'll want to be clear headed for the rest of the day. Won't you, Danny?"

Slim chuckled slightly, then said, "I believe I do, Mom."

Mae said, "Good. This is the day to mourn our loss, and there will be no more talk of death…. today."

On the Homestead Ranch, laziness was the call of the day, memories were being brought to mind, sadness at their loss, brief escapades of laughter mingled with grief of sudden removal of a loved one. Although Jenny and Mae make cakes, pies and cookies to keep their minds busy, there was no one in the house to devour, or even make a dent in the baked goods they had made. Mae, and Jenny stood in the kitchen staring at the amount of baked goods they had baked, and simply shook their heads.

Mae said, "Way made too much, Jen." Chuckling to herself, she said, "I hope Riley Crenshaw and the cowhands have a sweet tooth. We sure do have a lot to give them."

Jenny replied, "Well, we can keep a cake, and a pie, can't we? They're good for a snack."

Mae answered, "Of course we can, Dear. I have a sweet tooth myself."

Then, both women's chuckle elevated into laughter. Just then, Slim walked into the kitchen for a fresh cup of coffee. When he saw what his mother and sister had made, Slim just couldn't believe his eyes.

Slim said, "This house smells like a bakery. Now, I know why. For land sakes, you two have been busy."

Mae replied, "A might."

Jenny asked, "Too much, huh?"

Slim answered, "I'd say so."

Mae then said, "We have only one thought 'bout that, Son. Riley Crenshaw and the cowhands, if you'd be so kind as to take these baked goods to the cattle camp tomorrow."

Jenny turned to look at the grandfather clock on the far wall. Time: six fifty three p.m. in the evening.

Jenny then said, "Near supper time, but, after all this baking we've done, Mom, I'm just not in the mood to cook supper."

Mae asked, "You hungry, Jen?"

Jen replied, "Not really, no."

Mae turned to Slim asking, "How 'bout you, Son? You hungry?"

Slim answered, "I'm like Jenny, Mom, but a piece of cake and pie will do me good for the night."

Mae then said, "I feel the same as you two, but I'll only have a piece of pie, then I'm off to bed."

It was near nightfall when the Homestead went silent for the night. However, it seemed Slim, nor Jenny was tired enough to retire for the night. Mae had become tired with a heavy heart and a piece of rhubarb pie, then she retired to her bedroom. There were two rooms lit in the house. The living room, and the other was in Mae's bedroom. Slim sat in his father's chair by the fireplace. He picked up his father's pipe and pouch of tobacco. They were lying there on the end table away from the fireplace.

Jenny smiled, then said, "I'm goin' to miss smellin' that tobacco in the house."

Slim replied. "I find it strange that he didn't smoke the pipe when he was outside. He only smoked it in the house." Sounding confused, he asked, "I wonder why?"

Jenny replied, "I think I do." She smiled then said, "He did so to please Mother."

Slim said, "That thought never occurred to me, Jen."

Jenny then said, "You know what she has always used to say. It made her think of Grandpa, and she loved Dad for doin' it."

Slim looked at the name of the tobacco on the pouch. It read, 'Scotty's Butternut Burley Blend'.

He opened the pouch and took a whiff.

He shook his head slightly saying, "Oh, wow! A lot stronger aroma in the pouch than what swirls 'round in the air, let me tell you."

Jenny then said, "Well, I believe I'll be goin' to bed, Danny. It's been a tryin' day. I feel all wore out because of Dad's funeral. I'll take fresh flowers up to Dad tomorrow, and visit a while. That is if I can muster the strength." She rose from her chair saying, "Good night, Danny."

"You're a strong, young woman, Jenny. You can handle that just fine. Good night."

Chapter Seven

Long Distant Assassin

The next morning, as the dark clouds gave way to the light, the sun shown bright in the territory. At the Homestead, the moon shadows disappeared as they crept their way into the Nether land. Roosters crowed and fluttered their wings at the morning light. The farm animals were crowed awake, as well as the Siringo family from out of their soft down feather beds, as they lay underneath a bare minimum of a light cotton blanket, along with a down feather pillow, or two. It was the beginning of a new day. This is the day where all things old have now become new under the sun of a new day. A new outlook on life sprang into existence, and a different overall attitude was the premise of the day. Jenny was preparing breakfast just past daybreak. Coffee set to boil with the aroma permeating through the house. Eggs, buttermilk biscuits, and sausage gravy cooking on the stove.

The aroma of coffee caused Mae to come from her bedroom and meander into the kitchen, then reach into the cupboard for a cup. Behind her came Slim, also reaching for a cup.

Jenny smiled sweetly saying, "Sit down you two. Breakfast is just 'bout ready."

Mae yawned, then said, "Now, don't you sound lively, and energetic this mornin'."

Still half asleep, Slim then asked, "Yeah. What gives, Jen?"

As both Mae and Slim poured themselves a cup of coffee, Slim said, "This coffee smells so good."

"I agree, Son." Mae said, "Probably tastes good too. So, Jennifer, what makes you feel like you can take on the world this mornin'?"

Jenny replied, "I don't know, Mom. I just do. Can't say why though. I feel as fresh as a daisy this mornin', and I'm in good spirits too, thank you."

A few seconds later, the platter of biscuits was placed on the table, as well as the bowl of sausage gravy, and the plate of eggs, and the pot of coffee. Then, butter was placed on the table. As Mae's eyes took in the food that was set on the table, she smiled.

Mae said, "Smells delicious, Dear. Thank you for makin' breakfast."

Slim then said, "Looks good enough to eat, Jenny."

Jokingly, Jenny replied, "Well, I would hope so, Danny. Just listen to him, Mom. I'm a good cook, and he knows it too."

After Slim took a sip of his coffee, he said, "I'm just funnin' you, Jen. This food looks delicious."

Jenny sat down at the table saying, "Thank you."

Each grabbed a couple of eggs, as well as a couple biscuits. Each person broke open their biscuits and buttered each section, then they poured a ladle of gravy over the biscuit sections. Just as each one had taken a bite of food, there came the sound of many horses' hooves into the courtyard of the Homestead.

Mae asked, "Who is that, I wonder?"

Slim swallowed his bite of food, then quickly took a sip of coffee, then said, "I'll go see."

Slim excused himself as he left the table. He went into the living room and parted the curtain, as he looked out of the front window. When he saw who it was, he couldn't believe his eyes.

Just above a whisper, Slim said, "Well, I'll be."

He left the window and went to the door. He grabbed his hat, but left his gun belt hanging.

As Slim opened the door and went out onto the porch, the men who rode into the courtyard of the Homestead dismounted.

Slim, then yelled out, "Where in thunder have you fellas been? You just disappeared without a trace of any one a ya."

Walt answered, "Well, we're back."

Chuckling, Slim said, "I see that. So, who's there with you?"

Walt replied, "Friends. They came to help you get rid of Wade. We took off lookin' for 'em. We knew you needed more help than what we could give, so we found some. There's a few more comin', but they were some distance away. They should be here in a couple days, or so."

Slim shyly replied, "I appreciate this, Walt, but I can't afford…"

Walt, butted in saying, "Who said anything 'bout that? I didn't."

Confused, Slim asked, "They can't go up against hired gunmen without some kind a pay for doin' so. It ain't logical. It ain't right, either. I can't ask them to…"

"You don't have to." Walt replied. "I already have, and, as you can see, they have agreed. Satisfied?"

Slim answered, "Well, yes, but why?"

Walt replied, "Like I said, they're here to help you get rid of Devlin Wade. You ain't the only ones he has threatened, and even hurt. He's a scourge and he needs to be done away with, and these fellas have agreed to do just that."

Slim then said, "I really don't know what to say, Fellas."

Creel smiled saying, "Just say thanks, and we'll call it even."

Slim replied, "Sounds like somethin' I can't afford not to do. Thanks….?"

Creel answered, "The name's Creel. Just Creel."

Slim said, "Thanks, Creel. So, who are the others?"

Walt then said, "Well, let me introduce you." Pointing to Jonas, he said, "This is, Jonas Eberly."

Slim said, "Thanks, Mister Eberly."

"Just call me, Jonas, if you would."

"Alright, Jonas."

Then, Thaddeus stepped forward saying, "The name's, Thaddeus Doucet, out of Louisiana. New Orleans to be exact. Tis a pleasure to meet you, Monsieur Siringo."

As Slim smiled at the French language being spoken, Thaddeus put forth his right hand for a handshake. Slim shook his hand in friendship, and he shook it vigorously.

Slim replied, "Yes, well. Have you fellas had breakfast? Jenny made eggs, biscuits and gravy, and I believe she can make more."

Creel spoke saying, "Aw, no thanks. That camp cook of yours makes a perty good breakfast hisself."

Thaddeus then said, "Strangely enough, we had the same breakfast."

Jonas replied, "Down right tasty, it was too."

Walt said, "There should be three more men comin'. There should be a Jack Hardee, a Shane Garraty, and a Rafe Carson. They should be pullin' in here soon. They're good men, and we sure could use their help."

Slim answered, "You'll get no argument from me."

Thaddeus then said, "I fear we have interrupted Monsieur Siringo's breakfast. Of that, we apologize."

"I'm not worried 'bout that. It can always be re-heated." Slim replied. "I would invite you in, but you already had breakfast, and we're not really ready for company just now."

Walt replied, "That's understandable, Slim."

Creel then said, "We're sure sorry to hear 'bout your father, and him dyin' like he did."

Slim said, "It was a great loss to all a us. Doc said his heart gave out. Heart attack he called it, and yes, we buried him yesterday. The family and I are not ready for company."

Creel replied, "We understand. We came in yesterday, but then, we heard you buried your dad yesterday, so we spent the night at your cow camp. You have quite a few cows."

Slim replied, "A few, but still growing. If you will excuse me, gentlemen, I must return to my breakfast and my family. I will talk to you later today if that is okay?"

Walt replied, "That'll be just fine, Slim. We have things to do ourselves yet. We thought you'd like to know you're not in this fight alone."

Creel then said, "You have friends you never knew you had, and more are on the way."

Slim replied, "So I have been told. Thank you." He smiled.

As Slim turned to go back into the house, Walt, and the men with him mounted their horses, then rode away from the courtyard of the Homestead. As he opened the door, he stopped, then turned to watch the men in the distance as they rode away from the Homestead at a high lope. Shaking his head as if confused, he entered the house, closing the door behind him.

When he entered the kitchen, Mae asked, "Who was that, Dear?"

"They were… friends, Mom." Slim answered. "Walt, Will, and Fletcher brought friends to help us get rid a Devlin Wade, and his guns for hire."

Surprised, Jenny asked, "Really?"

With skepticism, Mae asked, "Their friends, or our friends?"

Slim replied, "Both I believe. I was told more were coming."

Jenny asked, "Did they say how many?"

Slim answered, "I was told at least three more are comin', maybe more, who knows? All I know is, we can sure use the help."

Jenny then said, "Won't that be somethin'? Just think of it. Our own army."

Mae sighed heavily, then said, "Not what I wanted to hear, Jennifer. So much shootin', and killin'. It gets more depressin' each day from what I hear in the news these days."

Slim replied, "What else can we do, Mom? We've tried talkin' and that didn't work. We

tried lettin' things slide for way too long. There has to be a day of reckoning for Wade. He just can't continue to run rough shod over people, plus, he can't continue to maim, and murder to steal other people's property just to satisfy his own lust for destruction for his own profit."

Jenny then said, "I'll re-heat your breakfast. It won't take long."

"Thanks, Jenny." Slim answered.

Jenny replied, "No problem. I'll make you some new coffee."

Mae then said, "What you said reminds me of somethin' I heard a long time ago. I nearly forgot the sayin' until just now when you mentioned Wade's own profit."

Slim said, "What's that, Mom?"

Jenny placed the coffee pot on the stove to make a new pot, "Yeah, tell us, Mom."

Jenny, then poured a little milk in the skillet to release the congealed gravy, and listened.

Then Mae replied, "I haven't heard this sayin' since I was just a young'un. That should tell you how long it's been around. Well, anyways, the sayin' goes somethin' like this, 'An evil man will burn his nation to the ground to rule over the ashes'."

Amazed, Slim breathed out, "Wow. What a statement."

Jenny replied, "Yep. That sounds like somethin' Wade would do. Guaranteed."

"I believe they have something planned already." Slim said. "I just don't know what that is … yet, but I will soon enough."

Jenny then said, "Well, whatever it is, it has to be good for us, right?"

Slim answered, "I would hope so, Jenny. I surely hope so."

Mae asked, "I wonder... can you trust those men you spoke of, Danny? We don't know anything 'bout them whatsoever."

Slim answered, "Well, if Walt, Fletcher, and Will trusts them, then I see no reason for us not to trust them."

Mae then said, "Well, they say that proof is in the puddin'."

Jenny added, "And, actions speaks louder than words."

"I got it. I got it." Slim retorted. "We'll just have to wait and see what they do, is all. I'm perty sure Walt will have his eyes on them as well." Then, as an afterthought, he said, "I hope." Jenny, then said, "So do I, Danny. So do I."

Slim said, "It could be that I could be gettin' closer to the man that uses hexagon bullets."

"What was the rifle he uses again, Danny?" Mae asked.

Slim answered, "It's a Whitworth Hexagon caliber .451 sniper rifle. It's a single shot muzzle loader. It's accurate at 2000 yards, even farther if using a scope."

Mae shook her head saying, "Strange rifle configuration with a bullet to match."

Slim sighed heavily, then said, "Long distant assassin. That's all it is. Not carin' who dies, or how a man dies, just as long as the man dies."

Mae replied, "From what I read in the newspaper today, they're sayin' a shootin' war is comin'. Northern states against southern states, That particular rifle would come in mighty handy, wouldn't it?"

"Unfortunately, you'd be right, Mom." Slim answered. "A man wouldn't know what hit him, nor know where it came from. His worries in this life would be over."

Jenny said, "That would be unjust and murder, wouldn't it?"

Slim replied, "In a shootin' war, anything goes, especially a sniper rifle. As the sayin' goes, 'All's fair in love and war'. That type a rifle would come in mighty handy."

A few miles out from the walnut grove, Tim McFadden, Kevin Taylor, and Clancy Burrows, who was riding next to the wagon, was headed southeast of Waco, Texas with the weapons wagon on their way to Matagorda on the southeastern coast. The weapons are to be shipped by the clipper ship, 'Arby Dunn', bound for the freedom fighters in Ireland by the Fenian Brotherhood in collaboration with the Molly Maguires. They were in quite a hurry. Time was wasting. Time they couldn't afford to waste. It was getting near the time that the clipper ship 'Arby Dunn', was set to sail for the western coast of Ireland to the port of Galway with trade goods and bought supplies. Knowing that the weapons could be worth more than what they were originally paid for because there was a strong rumor of a shooting war to start in the states, but the guns will be sorely needed in Ireland to use against the British and the English Crown for a free Ireland.

As the weapons wagon rolled over the known roads, Kevin asked, "From where we are now, how far to Matagorda on the coast?

Tim answered, "Oh, from Waco itself, it's 'round 245, 50 miles I'd say."

Clancy replied, "That's a far piece, especially through Karankawa territory, which is a brother hood per say of the, Borrados, Pintos, the Rayados, and the Pelones. They are from the Hokan family."

Tim asked, "Hokan? What does that mean?"

"It'd take too long to explain it and still you wouldn't get it." Clancy replied. "Let's just say a mean bunch of injuns. Almost as mean as the Comanche, but not by much."

Tim and Kevin exchanged glances, then Tim asked, "Who are these… cranky Indians?"

Clancy answered, "The Karankawa Injuns. They roam southeast Texas all the way from Galveston to Corpus Christi. Big chunk a territory. Cranky ain

t the word for it. Like I said, mean bunch of Injuns. Lift your hair quicker than a hiccup."

"Just how far are we from the Karankawa territory?" Kevin asked.

"Oh, anywhere between here and the coast." Clancy replied. "Their travels are quite extensive. Just when you think they shouldn't be there, well, there they are."

Sarcastically, Kevin then said, "That's comfortin'."

Tim said, "First it was the Comanche, then the Apache, then the Kiowa, then the Caddo, and now you're tellin' us the Karankawa's. What next?"

"I'm a afraid to ask." Kevin said.

Clancy replied, "The Comanche, the Apache, and the Kiowa are farther north than where we are now. Those tribes travel closer to the border for border raids, and in central Texas. Yet, you do have the Caddo, the

Coahuiltecans tribe, and the Wichita's, as well as, Karankawa's in southern Texas."

Kevin said, "I do believe Texas has more Indians than they do white men."

Clancy chuckled, then said, "It sure do seem that way sometimes."

Tim asked, "Can you speak this Karankawa language if by chance we happen to come upon them in our travels?"

"The only language I'll be spoutin' is... run!" Clancy said

Kevin replied, "Run?"

Clancy said, "Absolutely. They don't do much talkin', mostly doin', if you know what I mean."

Tim replied, "I'm beginnin' to understand. Death without mercy."

Clancy then said, "Exactly. Without mercy."

Kevin said, "That's spooky, don't ya think?"

Clancy replied, "Spooky? Simply scares the Dickens out a those who comes up against them."

Kevin then said, "I can see why. Devilish."

There was silence between them for a span of maybe 20 minutes. Each man to his own thoughts.

As Tim handled the reins, he finally said, "I figure to skirt 'round Lott, and Rosebud, and then enter Cameron to resupply ourselves."

Clancy asked, "How far to Cameron? It's been a while since I been this way."

Tim answered, "From where we are now to Cameron? Oh, I figure it to be 'round 50, 55 miles, give, or take a mile."

"Well, every mile puts us father into Karankawa territory." Clancy said. "We also must realize that the U.S Army is in dire need of weapons of any kind in the event that this country should explode into a shootin' war. I have a feelin' they'll be searchin' every wagon on every road for weapons, and confiscate them, and most likely ask what side they are standin' with. North, or South?"

Kevin then said, "Well, hopefully we won't run into either one a them. The Army, or the Karankawa's. I don't want to have our guns confiscated, nor do I want to die."

"I surely will, Captain." Corporal Jensen replied. "I'll let Lieutenant Chapman know you and Captain Udall are on your way."

Captain Locke then said, "Before you go, Corporal, you and trooper Streat pick up a wounded man, and take them back to the column with you. It would sure be a big help."

Jensen replied, "Sure thing, Captain. No problem, Sir."

Both men removed their foot from the left side stirrup and then a walking wounded man stepped into the stirrup, and were helped up to sit behind Streat, and Jensen. Then, when the wounded men were secure, and ready to travel, the two men kicked their horses in the flanks and took off at a high lope.

Then Captain Udall yelled out, "Let's move out! We'll follow your lead, Captain."

There was no more talking in the ranks. They moved as quickly as possible with the wounded grumbling, grunting, groaning, and moaning due to their wounds. Captain Locke, then ordered those who were mounted, and had a wounded man, to take them quickly to the column, then return to the detachment to get more wounded men. The troopers with a walking wounded man obeyed the order, and kicked their horses in the flanks, taking off near a gallop at the jump. Soon, the only troopers left were those carrying the wounded who were unable to walk, and those men who were unconscious and were not expected to live. Too many men were left behind on that rocky outcrop. Good troopers who breathed their last engaging the enemy. When the Indians knew where the white eyes had gone, they themselves entered the canyon in pursuit of them. Their leader had sent braves, around about, to the other entrance of the canyon in hopes to stop them from escaping the canyon and trap them, then destroy them. As the Indians came onto the rocky outcrop, scalps were taken from dead troopers, and cheers were raised in doing so. Then, the Indians went in pursuit of the troopers into the canyon. Captain Locke had

the insight to understand that that might happen, so, he and Captain Udall quickly hurried the men along. It wasn't all that long until the Indians that were sent to stop them from escaping the canyon came swooping up on them as they screamed their warbling war whoops. It was a courageous attack, especially for ten Indians against two squads of cavalry, half of which was well armed. A few of the troopers were shot dead, but the skirmish lasted but a few minutes.

Then, all ten Indians were shot down to lay in the dirt… dead. Most of the dead troopers were those who were not expected to live, and a couple of the troopers who were not wounded.

Captain Udall then said, "I believe the rest a those savages are in the canyon

in pursuit of the troop."

Captain Locke agreed saying, "I think so too. We have to move and move fast. No time for lollygaggin'. Stragglers will be on their own."

Captain Udall, then said, "We've moved as fast as we could, Captain. You take the detachment and go on. Me and what's left of my troop will hold them off as long as we can so you can make your escape."

Captain Locke turned to Captain Udal saying, "Get your troop movin', Captain."

Captain Udall looked at Captain Locke with surprise, then said, "Thank you, Captain."

Captain Locke replied, "You're welcome, Captain."

Just then, the troopers on horseback came racing back to the detachment just after the attack with weapons at the ready looking to make a fight of it. When the troopers saw what was, they then picked up more walking wounded, and headed back to the column in a hurry. At both times, when they were offered a mount, both Captain Locke and Captain Udall denied the offer, only to foot it with the rest of the detachment. Then, a squad of Cavalry from the column came racing into the detachment led by 1st Sergeant, Gene Ralston. As the squad passed the detachment and took up rear defensive positions as mounted skirmishers, Sergeant Ralston reined in where Captains Locke and Udall were.

Sergeant Ralston, then reported, "Captain, we will defend the rear position until you are able to move freely, and without troubles, Sir."

Captain Locke replied, "I take it Lieutenant Chapman sent you?"

1st Sergeant Gene Ralston answered, "Yes, Sir. He became aware of your situation when the troopers came in with the walking wounded."

Captain Locke then said, "I see, Sergeant. I appreciate you taking up defensive positions on our rear guard, Sergeant. A great Army tactic in the field. Thank you."

"Think nothing of it, Sir. Just doin' my duty as I see it, Captain."

Captain Udall said, "Thank you, Sergeant. I appreciate your sense of duty."

"Thank you, sir."

Captain Locke turned to Captain Udall saying, "Let's get out a here, shall we?"

Captain Udal replied, "After you, Sir."

Obviously, because of the ten Comanche Indians who attacked the detachment, there are less troopers than there was before to make it home to their family and friends. Their life was lost in the performance of their duty to the United States Cavalry. A deep heartfelt regret pounded in the chest of Captain Udall as he so desperately retreated in order to save what was left of his command as they fought against the scourge of the Comanche, and of course, himself. He felt a great obligation to Captain Locke and his troopers for coming to their aid, and helping them to get away from the death stings of the Comanche. As for Private 1st Class Nelson Pitt who made it through the Comanche to find Captain Locke? He will be rewarded with corporal stripes on his sleeve, if and when, they get back to Fort Arbuckle. He felt a particular kind of pride serving with the character of such men with their devotion to duty, and to be able to command such men.

It wasn't long before the detachment was in sight of the column. The rear guards kept their position for the detachment as mounted skirmishers until the detachment was well in close to the column. 1st Lieutenant Chapman, then kicked his horse in the flanks, and took off at a high lope towards the incoming detachment. When he neared Captains Locke and Udall, he reined his horse to a halt, but he sat on a dancing horse.

Lieutenant Chapman then said, "It's good to see you, Captain. I had my worries."

Captain Locke replied, "We had ours too, Lieutenant."

"No doubt, Captain." Lieutenant Chapman said. "You are aware the reinforcements are but a few hours away, Sir?"

"I am, Lieutenant." Captain Locke answered. "They will be more than welcomed."

Captain Udall then said, "Lieutenant Chapman, thank you."

Lieutenant Chapman smiled, then answered, "You're welcome, Captain."

Captain Locke then said, "Captain Udall, this is, 1st Lieutenant Micah Chapman, my second in command."

"Glad to make your acquain'tance, Lieutenant." Captain Udall replied.

Lieutenant Chapman then said, "And, I you, Sir."

Captain Locke then asked, "Anything else to report, Lieutenant?"

"Yes, Sir. I have sent out troopers to catch up your mounts, Captain Udall."

Captain Udall replied, happily, "Well, now, that is good news, Lieutenant. I wasn't lookin' forward to walkin' all the way back to Fort Arbuckle. Thank you, again, Lieutenant."

1st Lieutenant Chapman replied, "You're very welcome, Sir."

Captain Locke then said, "Lieutenant, have trooper Streat, and Corporal, Jensen run as gallopers to find out where our re-enforcements are, and how soon they will arrive."

Lieutenant Chapman answered, "Yes, Sir."

Then, Captain Locke said, "And have Ned Grayson search ahead for danger."

Lieutenant Chapman replied, "Yes, Sir."

Lieutenant Chapman reined his horse away from Captain Locke and went in search of the three men Captain Locke mentioned. Once he found them, he gave them the order that was given by Captain Locke. Then, at the jump, the three men left the column, and soon their horses reached a high lope racing away from the column.

Once the three men had left the column, the wounded men were put on wagons. The mounts of the troop from Fort Arbuckle under the command of Captain Silas Udall had been rounded up after being scattered by the Comanche, but much to the chagrin of Captain Udall, there were too many empty saddles. Those horses were utilized for the walking wounded. Then, the order was given to move out. Slowly, but surely, the column moved out. The mounted troopers who formed the rear mounted skirmishers at the rear of the detachment, kept their position at the rear of the column. No order for that was given. They just took up those positions on their own, and without orders.

Captain Udall turned to Captain Locke asking, "They read your mind, Captain?"

Captain Locke turned to look at the rear mounted skirmishers. He smiled, but said nothing.

Trooper Carl Streat, and Corporal Wirt Jensen, came upon the re-enforcements commanded by Rolo Quimby, no less than ten miles from the column. As the two men came into view, Captain Quimby halted the company, and waited for the two men to stop, and then have Corporal Jensen to give his report.

When the two men reined to a halt, Captain Quimby said, "Report, Corporal."

Corporal Jensen replied, "Captain, this is trooper Carl Streat from Captain Locke's column, but, now, there is more than just the column, Sir."

Captain Quimby then said, "Oh?"

Trooper Streat replied, "Yes, Sir. There is Captain Udall from Fort Arbuckle and what's left of his command after a run in with the Comanche. They were in a hard and difficult spot. He lost most of his command, and Captain Locke felt obliged to rescue the captain and his men from those blood-thirsty savages, Sir."

Chapter Eight

Tense Moments

Devlin Wade came from his office at the rear of the Lucky Deuce saloon. He meandered over to the bar, and was looking around the saloon in search of something, or someone. Fred, the bartender, was bringing in casks of beer, rolling the casks to the storeroom, different types of whiskey, and rare wines, as well as bottles of champagne. He, then began to stock the shelves behind the bar with a few of the products he had delivered and received. When he finally noticed Wade walking over to the bar, Fred looked at Wade as he swiped his hands together, ridding himself of the dirt accumulated on the bottles and casks. He, then picked up a bar towel to wipe his hands of the residue.

Fred then said, "Mornin', Boss."

Without turning, Wade replied, "Mornin', Fred."

Fred asked, "What will be your pleasure this mornin'?"

Ignoring the question, Wade said, "If it wasn't for my own men and a couple a dandified card sharps, this place would be near empty. Cardsharps." He scoffed then said, "All fluff and stuff, but with worried eyes, if you know what I mean?"

"I do indeed, Boss, but I believe it's just nervous indigestion, myself." Fred said. "They do put a fright in me. They are just so calculated."

Wade replied, "It's their business, Fred. It's a game of calculated risks where death, or riches, may be waiting at the turn of a card." He turned back to the saloon, asking, "Have you seen Emmette Stone, and Aaron Morris this mornin'?"

"I haven't seen them this mornin'. They should be in later I would think." Fred replied.

Wade then said, "When you see them, let them know I want to see them. I have a chore for them to do for me."

Fred replied, "Will do, Boss. Anything else?"

Wade answered, "No. Not at the present."

Wade turned from the bar, walked across the saloon to a table where a card game was goin. The card game had been going since two days ago with no interruptions, except for the usual mother nature exceptions. Game play continued, so when and if a player returned to the table, he bought himself back in at table stakes. He didn't say anything not wanting to change the mood of play. He turned to go outside. As he went to pass a gambler playing solitaire, he stopped. Wade looked over the cards laying on the table.

Wade then said, "Red jack on black queen."

The gambler moved the red jack to the black queen.

Then, he looked up at Wade saying, "Thanks, Mister."

Wade didn't say anything, he just gave a nod of his head and kept walking. When he went through the swinging doors of the saloon to the boardwalk outside, the bright sunlight caused him to squint against the sunlight. He stopped, then pulled a cheroot from his inside jacket pocket. He, then struck a match and lit his cheroot. He took two to three puffs on his cheroot to make sure it was lit. He looked up and down the street just to see what was going on. His men were spread up and down the street with their rifles cradled in the crook of their arms, just in case trouble should it arise.

Sitting their horses on the outskirts of Comanche, Creel said, "Think I'll go into town and get a feel of the place, and get a lay of the land."

Walt then said, "Now, why would you do that? Take my word for it, Creel, I've met all manner of man in my life, but he is one of the most coldhearted men I have ever met."

Creel replied, "I've met the same kind a man at one time, or another. So, what's different 'bout him?"

"This fella will smile to your face as he plunges a knife in your back." Walt replied. "That's what makes him different from other men, I reckon. He's not a flighty kind a man either. He's decisive, and yet, reckless at the same time. Never trust a man such as that. It ain't healthy."

Then Thaddeus spoke saying, "From what you say 'bout the man, Walter, he makes my skin crawl. That isn't easy for me to admit."

Will then said, "I met him once, and he rubbed me the wrong way."

Fletcher said, "I agree with Will, Thad. The man is one of a kind. Cold blooded as a coiled rattle snake."

Thaddeus said, "How 'bout I go with you, Creel? I'd like to see this man for myself."

Creel replied, "Good idea, Thad. Let's take it slow to not attract attention. We'll be viewed as a possible threat when we hit town anyways."

Jonas Eberly then said, "I'll go along. Three men just might make a difference."

Creel said, "Could be you're right, Jonas. More eyes and ears are a welcome thing."

Walt replied, "If you're tryin' to get one of us to go in with you… No dice. We've already seen the man."

It was mid-morning when the three men left the outskirts of Comanche, and entered town ever under the watchful eyes of Wade's gunmen. As the three men rode the street, they noticed there wasn't many people walking the boardwalks. A couple of Wade's gunmen walked the boardwalk behind them at a distance. There was only one buckboard in town, and it was at Hoeble's Mercantile with a man in his thirties and his son of 15, or 16 was loading supplies on the buckboard. They also noticed a man on the run to the Lucky Deuce saloon. Probably to let Wade know there was company coming. The three men reined in at the Lucky Deuce saloon, then stepped down from their saddles. The men tethered their horses at the hitching rack in front. They entered the saloon and meandered over, and bellied up to the bar.

Fred asked, "What can I get you fellas?"

Each man ordered a beer. Fred, then filled the beer mugs from the beer dispenser, then set the beer mugs on the bar.

Fred then said, "That'll be six bits, Gentlemen."

Each man reached into their pockets, and then tossed a quarter on the bar.

As Fred lifted the quarters from the bar, he said, "Thank you, Gentlemen."

Fred opened the metal cash box under the bar, then tossed the quarters in it, then closed the box. All three men turned from the bar with their backs resting against the bar. They stood staring at the men in the card game taking place at a table some distance away from them. They also noticed the two men who had followed them step into the saloon. They, also, come to notice that men in the saloon, being Wade's gunmen, most of them, suddenly gave them special attention...

Then, there came a knock on Wade's office door.

Wade said, "Enter."

Erwine Brown opened the door and went in. Wade looked up as Erwine closed the door.

Wade asked, "What can I do for you, Erwine?"

Erwine replied, "Just thought you'd like to know, Wade, me and Keith Rachlin followed three cowboys into the saloon. They had… well, they had a look 'bout them that spelled out... not just cowboys, but could mean trouble."

Wade sat back in his chair saying, "Now, why should I trouble myself with these three cowboys? They're probably just passin' through and came in to cut the dust from their throats."

Erwine replied, "I just thought maybe you would be in'trested enough to have a talk with them fellas, and find out why they are here, is all."

"Tell you what you do, Erwine." Wade then said. "You and Keith Rachlin keep an eye on those three fellas, and if trouble does come up, then you two handle it in your own imaginative way."

Erwine speculated before saying, but then said, "You sure you want us to do that, Wade?"

Wade answered, "Why not? That's what you get paid to do, isn't it?"

Erwine replied, "Just makin' sure we could play a whole hand."

"You have my blessings, Erwine." Wade replied. "Do what you will."

"Keith will be glad to hear that, Wade."

Wade then said, "There's only two a you. Grab Ron Murchison to make it even."

Erwine said, "If you think it's best."

Wade replied, "I do. They just may get lucky, and I wouldn't like that."

"That ain't very encouraging, Wade." Erwine answered.

Wade chuckled a little, then said, "I never bet against the odds, Erwine. There is always the chance they can whittle away the odds, then I'd be out men I can use. Comprende?"

Erwine replied, "Yeah. I comprende." Then, spitefully Erwine said, "Thanks."

As Erwine walked to the door, he stopped, then turned back to give Wade a wicked stare.

Wade smiled, then remarked, "Good luck."

Angrily, "Yeah." Erwine replied. "Thanks again."

As the door to his office opened, then closed and latched, Wade shook his head and scoffed.

Out at the bar, Creel said, "Let's find a table." So, the three men found a table in the center of the saloon, and sat down. Then, Erwine came from the rear of the saloon to talk to Keith Rachlin.

When he came up to Keith, Erwine asked, "Any trouble?"

Keith answered, "No. No trouble. What did Wade have to say?"

"Wade said if these yahoos start any trouble, we can take care of it ourselves, and we can play the whole hand with his blessings."

Keith replied, "That's good to hear." He scoffed, then said, "Let's just see what these hombres are made of. They look awfully surly to me. Especially that big fella."

"Are you sure you want to do what I think you want to do?"

"Sure I'm sure." Keith answered.

"Well, they haven't started any trouble is what I'm sayin'. They may not be as pushable as you think they are. They just might push back."

As they walked off, Keith shrugged his shoulders saying, "So, let's find out."

"I'm not too sure 'bout this, Keith. Wade said if *they* start trouble."

"It'll be just fine, Erwine. Just follow my lead."

"Okay, but, I'm afraid I know where this will lead."

"You worry too much."

"Yeah, and I'm still alive because of it."

Then, there was silence between them as they walked over to the table where the three men sat.

As Creel took a sip of his beer, Keith asked, "You fellas just passin' through?"

Setting his beer mug down on the table, Creel looked up at Keith, then replied, "Yeah. Just passin' through. Why?"

Keith said, "Oh, no reason. Just askin'."

Jonas, then asked, "You the sheriff 'round here?"

Keith answered, "Who, me? Naw, I ain't the sheriff. Let's just say I'm a conscientious citizen of Comanche."

Thaddeus then said, "Well, Monsieur, you found out what you needed to know so…"

Keith butted in, then asked in a surly way, "So, you're tellin' me to mind my own business?"

Creel answered, "In a word, yes."

Keith turned to look at Erwine saying, "Well, what do we have here? We have a foreigner in our midst."

Keith and Erwine laughed. Then Jonas asked Fred for three more beers to come to the table. Fred filled the beer mugs from the dispenser, placed them on a tray, and then walked towards the table. Keith looked at Erwine and winked, then moved a couple feet from the table. When Fred had come parallel with Keith, Keith stuck his foot out, tripping Fred, causing Fred to fall, spilling the tray of beers all over the floor. Keith laughed wickedly.

Lying on the floor, wet and confused, Fred shouted, "What did you do that for, Keith?" As he stood to his feet, he said, "Now, look at what you done."

Creel, Jonas, and Thaddeus stood from the table in a huff.

Through his laughter, Keith then said, "Oops, I'm so sorry. I didn't...."

But he never finished his sentence because Creel, out of nowhere, hit Keith with a haymaker of a right hand, which sent Keith backwards over a nearby table to sprawl out on the floor.

Erwine then said, "I had a feelin' it would turn out like this."

Then, suddenly, Erwine took a swing at Creel, but Creel ducked. Then, Jonas hit Erwine in the midsection doubling him over, then, Thaddeus hit Erwine with a straight downward fist, sending him to the floor all crumpled up in an almost curled up position. Wade's gunmen in the saloon stood quickly to their feet, wondering if this is what Wade ordered, or if it was a personal fight.

Thaddeus said, "I suggest we now leave, Creel."

Creel replied, "I think you're right, Thad."

The three men started backing out of the saloon. They did not draw their weapons, but there were tense moments between them and Wade's gunmen. The three men thought that gunfire would erupt at any minute. They wondered if they would even make it to the swinging doors without getting shot. They stepped backwards to the swinging doors around tables and chairs, then they stepped through the doors to the boardwalk. They quickly turned to the street, untethered their horses, mounted their horses, and rode quickly out of town to where Walt, Fletcher, and Will were waiting. When the three men got to Walt, Fletcher, and Will waited, they reined their horses to a halt. Walt, Fletcher, and Will were waiting in the shade of a Red Maple tree.

The three men dismounted and walked over to them.

Walt, then asked, "Well?"

Creel replied, "We never did see this, Devlin Wade fella, but we did have a little trouble with a couple of his gunmen."

Walt replied, "Well, I see you made it out in one piece."

Thaddeus then said, "True enough, Monsieur, but there were tense moments. We were lookin' at eight to ten well-armed men, and I'm guessing all were Wade's men."

Creel chuckled saying, "The air was thick with suspense. Those men didn't know if they should start shootin', or not. We backed out gracefully with no problem, and here we are."

Jonas said, "Each step we took was a great relief, which meant we were still walkin'.'"

Will said, "Unfortunately, you didn't see the big man himself. He has a dry wit, and a cold disposition 'bout him. Gave me the willies just to 'round him."

Fletcher then said, "He's a man of his own making for sure. He's calculated, cunning, treacherous, and frightfully scary."

Will added, "And, he's hated by everyone in Stephens County, except his hired guns. Those who are still alive that is. He's proclaimed himself, 'King', of Stephens County."

Creel replied, "So, this man Wade has murdered, stole cattle, pushed people off their land by hook, or by crook, jumped claims." He paused, then asked, "What kind of claims?"

Walt answered, "You name it, Creel. His greed is bigger than his ego, and his ego is quite large. He thinks very well of himself."

Creel said, "Well, I believe it's time to de-throne this self-made king. Now that we know what we're up against, and the kind a man that he is. We need to work out a plan and then see it through."

Walt then said, "How 'bout we wait for those who are comin', and have them see what we're up against, and then make a plan?"

Thaddeus said, "How 'bout we make a plan, and then they can listen to the plan, and then they can put the finishin' touches to it."

Walt took his pocket watch from his vest pocket, pushed the pin and the cover sprang open.

Checking the time, he said, "Ten-thirty. I figure by the time we get to the cattle camp on the Homestead Range, it should be time for afternoon eats."

Thaddeus added, "Quite true. Monsieur Crenshaw sure cooks good. He makes a good cup a tea too."

Then, all six men reined their horses from Comanche and headed for the cattle camp of the Homestead ranch. There was little to no conversation between them. As they reined in at the cattle camp, Riley Crenshaw has finished preparing his noon meal. He, then grabbed a metal rod, and began to ring a metal triangle designed to gather cowhands signifying food is ready. The men from the cattle camp, and the men who just came in, stepped down from their saddles. They each walked over to where the plates and silverware were and took up each. Lunch was chili-with beans, Johnnie cake. Dessert was Indian Pudding, which is a warm baked custard made with milk, cornmeal, molasses, and cinnamon. It's dandy for a cowboy's sweet tooth.

Eric Pendergast sat down on the tongue of the wagon wheel after taking his plate and silverware to the pot of soapy water, but he refilled his coffee cup. He then brought out a newspaper and began reading.

Creel noticed, then walked over to Eric, asking, "Where'd you get that?"

Eric replied, "I've had it a while."

Creel chuckled saying, "Keepin' up with the times, are ya?"

Erick replied, "This old rag? It's two weeks old. We don't get the paper all that often, and I do love to read."

Creel then said, "What are they sayin' 'bout the shootin' war they say is comin'?"

Erick answered, "What's bein' said is that the shootin' war is inevitable and will come sooner than what people think, and to be prepared for what's comin'."

Creel then asked, "How does one get prepared for war?"

Erick answered, "Choose your allegiance, I suppose. Fight for what you believe in and hope what you're fightin' for is the right reason, and choose the way of life you will fight for."

Creel replied, "Could be you're right. Does that paper say, or at least give a hint as to when that shootin' war could start?"

Erick replied, "Naw, no dates. Not even a time of year. It only says it is inevitable to start at any time. Tsk, tsk, tsk. They say Congress is divided on the issue of slavery, and of course the southern states are saying that the institution of slavery, and that way of life it affords is sacred to the south. They argued that each state was a single individual state with its own Constitution long before we became the United States, and, so, they say they have the right to secede from the Union and discard the Constitution if they so desire."

Jonas and Thaddeus walked up and leaned against the wagon wheel, and stood listening to what Erick, and Creel was talking about.

Creel then said, "Is that what they're sayin'? Disregard the Constitution? Are you sure?"

Pointing to the paper, Erick replied, "It's right here in black and white."

Jonas then said, "Ain't that somethin'? We could be livin' on the precipice of a civil war. If it does come as the say it will, it will be remembered 50-100 years from now, even longer."

Riley said, "Hist'ry books will be filled with it… forever I think."

Walt then said, "It'll be a hist'ry makin' event for sure. American against American, instead of American against the British, or any other foreign power."

Thaddeus replied, "As it says in La Bible, 'A house divided against itself cannot stand'. Surely those people in the Capitol, and the Congress has considered that fact?"

Riley then said, "Well, time will tell when that shootin' war starts. Then, that will mean they care nothin' 'bout the United States Constitution."

Creel lifted his coffee cup and stared at it, then walked away saying, "If that happens, many, many graves will need to be dug."

Will then said, "And, the loss of life will be tremendous. That's a scary thought."

Fletcher added, "That would mean the United States would be divided into two nations. Now, that's scary, if you was to ask me."

Creel had walked over to the coffeepot hanging from a hook attached to a skewer rod over the campfire. He poured himself a cup of coffee as the wranglers of the Homestead crew mounted their horses, and rode away from the cattle camp headed for the herd.

Instead of going to the herd with the rest of the crew, Mike Eagan pointed the nose of his horse towards the Siringo house. Sheriff Matt Tucker also nosed his horse to the Siringo house. When they got there, they found Slim at the corral, saddling his horse.

When they had halted their horses near the corral, Matt said, "Where ya goin'?"

Slim replied, "Oh, I thought to go huntin'."

Mike then said, "Huntin'? How long? A day, or two? You haven't enough supplies for no more 'n that."

Slim answered, "All depends on what you're huntin."

Tossing his right leg around the saddle horn, Matt said, "Okay, I'll bite. What causes you to go huntin' for a day, or two, all by your lonesome?"

Slim turned to the duo saying, "A man who carries a certain type of rifle with a certain type of bullet. That's who I'm huntin'."

Mike said, "Come again."

Matt then said, "Slim's brother Randy was killed by a hexagon bullet, so, Slim here, he's goin' in search of the man who carries that rifle that uses that type a bullet, but he's known 'bout that hexagon bullet for quite some time now, so, why now? Ever thought of askin' for help just in case you should need it? You know as well as I do, you can't go into Comanche and come out alive. You'll be carried out feet first if you do."

Slim replied, "I have been lettin' that bullet escape my memory for far too long. It's time I went huntin' for the man who carries that rifle and put him down."

Matt replied, "I agree that the man needs to be put down, but you goin' alone is like signing your own death certificate. You know Wade hates the sight of you, and when he finds out you're in town every one a his gun hands will be after your hide."

Slim then said, "I have to try, Matt." As he stepped into the stirrup, he repeated, "I have to try."

Slim, then swung himself onto the saddle.

As Slim situated himself, Mike said, "Now, hold on, Slim. Don't go off half-cocked."

"Jenny said the same thing, Mike, but I have my head on straight." Slim replied.

Just then, the sound of horses' hooves pounding the soft ground as they came onto the Homestead.

All three men turned their heads in the direction of the coming horses' hoofbeats.

As the men rode into the courtyard, Slim asked, "Wonder what they want?"

As the men came into the courtyard and neared the corral, they halted their horses.

Walt, then asked, "Where you fellas off to?"

Matt replied, "He says he's goin' huntin'."

Mike then said, "Yeah. Huntin' a man with a sniper rifle who uses a hexagon bullet."

Jonas said "A hexagon bullet? I ain't never heard of such a thing?"

Thaddeus then replied, "I have."

Slim became real interested in what Thaddeus Doucet had to say about that hexagon bullet and the rifle who uses it.

What Slim wanted, no, what he needed to know was the name of the man who uses that type of rifle.

Thaddeus said, "That type a rifle, Monsieur, is a Whitworth caliber .451 single shot muzzle loader sniper rifle. Am I correct?"

Slim stared at Thaddeus with a hard stare, then said, "You are quite correct. Not many have been made, well, from what I've been told. A friend of mine had one, but as far as I know he's not in the territory, and I don't honestly believe he would do something like murder."

Creel said, "You'd be surprised what a man would do for money, even murder just to survive these days."

Slim asked, "So, Thaddeus, do know who that man is, and could he be here?"

Thaddeus replied, "He could, Monsieur, as well as, your friend who has one. It could also be someone completely unknown to both a us. Nothin' is beyond the pale of reality."

Slim, then asked, "Perhaps you could tell me the man's name?"

Thaddeus replied, "Jubal Todd is the man I speak of. He is the one who has one a those rifles. Now, whether, or not he is in the territory, and if he is the man you're lookin' for, that is a big if, Monsieur."

Slim said, "Are you sure of that name, Thaddeus?"

"As sure as I know my own name, Monsieur."

Then a very worried look crossed Slim's face. He then stepped down from the saddle, tethering his horse to the middle rung of the corral of the three rung fence.

The other men dismounted as they were wondering what took hold of Slim in a much worried countenance.

Matt then asked, "So, Slim, what has got you so worried?"

Mike then said, "Yeah. You look almost heartsick."

Slim had a worried, faraway look on his face. He replied a few seconds later.

Slim said, "That's the name of that friend I mentioned who had one of those rifles. It has been quite a while since I seen him last, but he could've become proficient with that weapon, but not murder. I find that hard to believe."

Thaddeus then said, "Maybe we're talkin' 'bout two different people. Your friend could've gone by a different name for some reason."

Slim then asked, "Wonder what that reason could be? An outlaw?"

Thaddeus replied, "I don't know, but the man I know is cold-hearted. He'd gut you like a fish while he's laughin' at you. He has two beady eyes. Wears a crooked smile. He has a scar on his right cheek 'bout an inch long, anglin' down to the right when you're lookin' at him. He stand 'bout six-two, six-four in boots, with dirty blonde hair spllin' out from under his hat"

Slim sighed, then said, "Yeah, I know. The scar he carries I gave him some time back." He sighed again. "I can't believe it's him. Jubal Todd. I never would a thought it was him." Slim sighed, then said, "If it is him, why haven't we met here recently? We were good friends once upon a time. At least I thought we were."

Matt then said, "Could be he's only needed for somethin' special, like your brother, Randy."

Creel then said, "He must've known he was your brother, right? After all, your last name, Siringo, is not all that familiar anywhere."

Slim said, "Jubal knew of Randy. He knew of him alright. I spoke of Randy often." He sighed heavily, then said, "What would cause a man, such as I thought Jubal was, to turn to doin' what he's doin'?"

Creel said, "Why are you in such an all fired hurry to get yourself hurt, or killed by tryin' to do this thing yourself? Remember, you have friends to help you, plus, we have more men who are comin in a day, or two, to help get rid of Wade. So, why not wait until they get here, then, we can come up with a plan to do just that?"

Slim replied, "Don't you think I've waited too long as it is?"

Matt answered, "I know how you feel, Slim, but, what's a day, or two more? You've waited this long. Besides, it may turn out to be the right thing done in just a few days."

Mike then said, "Do yourself a favor and wait till we have everyone together."

"Can you be sure these men are comin?" slim asked.

Walt replied, "I received a telegram from Garrick Lattigo stating they would be coming. It would take a day, or two for them to get here. So, as far as I know, they are on their way."

When that was said, Slim opened the corral gate, led his horse inside, and began to unsaddle his horse. As he placed the saddle blanket, the saddle, and gear over his shoulder, he headed for the barn.

Surprised, Fletcher then asked, "Does that mean he's goin' to wait?"

Matt gave a sigh of relief, then said, "I think so. I truly think so."

Chapter Nine

Misbehaving

Meanwhile, in Comanche, Seth Brubaker, half owner of the Silver Shovel Silver Mine was prowling the back alley headed for the saloon. He moved in the shadows, keeping a sharp eye out for Wade's hired gunmen. He went to hiding when one, or two of Wade's gunmen came walking the alley ways. He had a score to settle with Devlin Wade since it was Wade who gave the order to have his partner, Amos Stegner, shot and killed. Seth himself was hunted, but was never found, so it was thought he had left the country, leaving Wade to make his claim on the silver mine with no one to contest it. Well, as sure as the day is long, he will get his revenge.

When he finally reached the back entrance to the saloon, he heard rustling from inside the storeroom. Then, the door opened, causing Seth to quickly seek a hiding place. Fred was tossing a pan of soapy water out of the back door into the alley. As Fred was closing the door, Seth quickly jumped from his hiding place, and sprang to the door, putting a piece of wood against the door post keeping the door from closing. When the door wouldn't close, Fred turned to find out why, then found what was keeping the door from closing. So, he bent down to remove the piece of wood from against the doorpost. He was wondering how it got there, and that's when the lights went out because Seth clubbed him over the head with the butt of the rifle. Fred landed hard, and unconscious, half in and half out of the doorway. Seth leaned his rifle against the outside wall of the saloon, then he dragged Fred from the doorway. He made sure the piece of wood against the door post would keep the door from closing. When he laid Fred away from the door, he made sure Fred was breathing and wasn't dead. There was only one man he wanted to see dead, and he wanted to be the one to cause his demise, and that man was Devlin Wade.

Seth then entered the storeroom of the saloon and found himself in a room full of unopened alcoholic beverages. He stared longingly at the beer bottles lining the walls, along with whiskey bottles, the wine bottles, and the beer kegs located around the room, as well as, bottles of champagne wine, but to hear him tell it, he never much cared for the taste of champagne wine. He, then remembered why he broke into the storeroom. Kill Devlin Wade. His eyes narrowed with determination as he went to the door that led to the main room. Since he and Amos had been in the Lucky Deuce at least twice before, Seth knew where Wade's office was located. He opened the door and looked around. He knew the hallway to the left was where he needed to go. His hope was that Wade was in his office, and not out in the bar area. Stealthily, he crept down the hall towards Wade's office, looking ahead, and behind him. Closer, and closer he got to Wade's office door. Finally, he came up to it. His hands began to sweat for he had never killed a man before in his life, but Wade had caused the death of his friend and partner, Amos Stegner, and to his way of thinking, it was fitting that Wade met the same fate that he had in mind for both he and Amos. Seth, himself barely escaped the fate that Amos had suffered. The following day, Seth had come from his hiding place in the rocks above the silver mine where he had escaped to and went into hiding. Seth looked around the area, and he eventually went over to where the body of Amos was located. Sadness crept over him as he stared at the body of his friend and partner. He finally gathers his courage, and he buries his friend and partner. As he stood over the grave of Amos, he vowed a vow of revenge against Devlin Wade even if it caused his own demise. Thus, his reason for being in the Lucky Deuce saloon with a rifle in his hands.

Wade was sitting at his desk doing some figures of the profits from the night before when the door flung open. He turned quickly to see Seth Brubaker pointing a rifle at him. He looked horrified as he stared down the barrel of a Henry repeating rifle. Before he was able to react to this death proposal, a shot rang out. Seth Brubaker flinched greatly to the impact of the bullet, grabbing the door post after dropping his rifle, he crumbled into Wade's office to lie dead on the floor. It was then that Wade sprang from his chair at his desk. He backed up quickly as Seth fell to the floor. The Henry repeating rifle skidded across the floor. Wade wiped his mouth with his hanky as he grabbed from the pocket square in his suit. Wade stared in wide-eyed wonderment. A few seconds later, Fred, the bartender, stood in the doorway with a smoking .45 caliber revolver in his hand. Wade stared at Fred as he stood in the doorway of his office.

Wade then said, "Well, at least we now know he didn't leave the country." He continued to wipe his face and brow. "Whew! How did you know he was here to kill me?"

Fred replied, "Í didn't. When I came to, I was out in the alley. I was clubbed from behind, and it took a few minutes to clear the cobwebs. When I came in to I headed for the bar, then I noticed he was lurking near your office. That's when I knew who it was, and what he was plannin' to do."

Wade asked, "How did you know what he was plannin' to do?"

Fred replied, "Because I would've done the same thing if it was me."

"I suppose you would've, wouldn't you?" Wade replied. "When that door flung open, all I could see was a rifle barrel aimed at me, and I thought I was breathing my last."

Then, the hallway quickly became crowded with people who heard the gunshot, and came running to find out who fired it with their own weapons drawn. A few men entered Wade's office to see who it was got shot. They all stared at the body in disbelief. Then, as soon as it was known who the dead man was, the name, Seth Brubaker, was passed around through the crowd in a lively, and excited chatter.

One man in the crowd yelled out, "Hey, don't he and this… oh what's his name?"

Another man hollered, "Amos Stegner."

"Yeah, Amos Stegner." The first man replied. "Don't this Amos Stegner, and this feller here own the Silver Shovel silver mine?"

Wade then said, "Well, this man, Seth Brubaker, snuck in here and tried to kill me, but, thanks to Fred here, he died tryin'."

The commotion continued in the hallway with wild, undiscernible, overlapping chatter.

Wade finally said, "Somebody help get this body out a my office and take it over to Rose's funeral home, then have someone clean up this mess."

Fred replied, "I'll have it cleaned up in no time a'tall, Boss, once the body is removed."

As men picked up the body of Seth Brubaker, Wade, said, "No, you won't, Fred."

Fred looked at Wade confused, asking, "I won't?"

Wade answered saying, "No, you won't. I'll have someone else clean this mess up. You saved my life, Fred. I'll not forget that."

Without realizing it, a smiled spread across Fred's face as he said, "Thanks, Boss."

When Tim McFadden, Kevin Taylor, and Clancy Burrows skirted the community of Rosebud, Texas it was mentioned that Cameron was only 15, to 16 miles farther on. The question was brought up by Tim, should they go on, and enter the town of Cameron, Texas at, or near sundown, and sleep in a soft bed in the hotel, if possible, and have breakfast in a diner, or, should they spend the night on the prairie, and have supper, and breakfast with whatever they have between them, and then enter Cameron during the morning hours when businesses, including the diner, would be open for business? It was therefore agreed by Kevin and Clancy both that they would continue on to Cameron. It was a half hour before sundown when they entered the town of Cameron, Texas. The Livery was easy enough to find. Tim brought the wagon to a halt in front of the Cobb Livery.

Hearing the noise of the wagon, Parley Cobb, the owner of the Livery, walked outside to see what was up.

Parley asked, "What can I do for you, fellas?"

Tim answered, "We'd like to leave this wagon in your hands, Lad. We've traveled far and in dire need of rest and refreshments. Our animals deserve the same. Treat them well, Sir."

The Livery owner replied, "They call me, Cobb, Parley Cobb. I own this Livery, and I always treat horses well, sometimes better 'n most folks I know."

Tim, then said, "Meanin' no disrespect, Mister Cobb. Could you be so kind as to tell us where the hotel is in this hamlet?"

"Hamlet?" Parley replied as he chuckled. "Cameron is no hamlet, Mister, but it's a clean, easy goin', friendly town."

Tim, said, "As I said, Mister Cobb, no offense. Where is the hotel located?"

Parley replied, "Just down the street on your left. Eatin' place is, Bivins Diner, next door. Hattie Bivins sure sets a fine table, let me tell you." He chuckled merrily, then said, "Larrupin' good stuff."

Kevin asked, "So, my good man, how much would it be to retain your services?"

"Depends." Parley replied.

Clancy asked, "On what?"

Parley answered, "How long you plan on stayin'."

Kevin replied, "We should be leavin' your burg just after breakfast tomorrow mornin'."

Parley then said, "In that case… would five dollars be worth my while?"

Tim answered, "That would fine, Lad. If you have any questions, you'll find us in the pub havin' a pint."

Parley said, "I take it you mean the saloon havin' a beer?"

Kevin chuckled, then replied, "Aye, that we do. I believe we can find that establishment on our own."

Parley then said, "I have no doubt."

Tim took his wallet from his inside coat pocket and handed Parley a five dollar bill, then added another dollar for good measure."

Parley took the bills, then said, "Uh, you have paid me too much, Sir."

Tim then said, "On purpose, Sir. Your kindness is to be rewarded."

As the sun began to sink below the horizon, Tim, Kevin and Clancy found their way to the hotel, and registered for the night. They, then headed to the saloon for a beer to wash the dust out of their throats, and quench their thirst. When they entered the saloon they found it near empty, but for five men who looked like a bunch of rough and rowdy men. These were not the type of men to take lightly. They looked like it wouldn't take much to get their ire up. There was maybe three townsmen of Cameron in the place who were keeping their distance from these men. Those men were sitting at a table near the swinging doors for an easy escape if need be. It was time to be on their best behavior, or they would find more trouble than they can handle. The rough, and rowdy looking men were vulgar and noisy in their whiskey drinking. They were slapping each other on the back, and airing their lungs (cursing) with no respect for others.

When Tim, Kevin, and Clancy got to the bar they each ordered a beer. It then became quiet. Tim, Kevin, and Clancy turned to find out why there was no more rowdy noise, and when they did, they noticed that the five men were staring at them crudely.

Tim said, "Ignore them, Lads. We've done nothing to warrant any kind a trouble with these men. So, don't do anything to cause attention."

Kevin replied, "Tis easier said than done I fear, Me bucko. Tis our Irish brogue that has grabbed their attention. I fear our manner of speech has put us in trouble with these men."

Clancy stared at the men who were staring at them, then said, "Now, how could we be in trouble with these men when we haven't said, nor done anything to deserve any trouble?"

Kevin replied, "By the looks on their faces it wasn't hard to do, Lad."

One of the rowdy men stepped forward saying, "Well, now, lookie what we got here." He chuckled eerily, then said, "We have foreigners in our midst. Now, I ask you, why do we have foreigners in our midst?"

Tim said, "We're not lookin' for trouble, Mister. We just want to drink our pint of ale in peace, and then we'll be leavin'."

"Pint of ale he says." The man scoffed. "That is beer in a beer mug. Not a pint of ale. Why is it you foreign nut jobs think you can just come waltzin' in here and act like you own the place?"

Tim asked, "Whatever gave you that idea, Mate? We came in here after a long dusty ride to quench our thirst, and we're not lookin' for trouble. So, please, allow us that courtesy."

A second man, then said, "Are you sassin' him, Boy! Reese don't like it when somebody sasses him, and neither do I."

Reese said, "Thanks, Homer. Bein' sassed does grate on me some. It causes me to have an unfriendly attitude."

Just then, the bartender said, "Now, hold on fellas. I don't want no trouble in my place.

So, take it outside and settle it."

One of the townsmen recognizing trouble slipped out of the saloon in a hurry to fetch the sheriff.

The bartender then said, "I know for a fact that the sheriff will be here any minute, so, you fellas shake hands, and be friends, or you can leave my establishment."

Another rowdy man said, "Friends? With these foreigners? Ha! Never."

The bartender, then said, "What offense have they done to you? None. So, let's not have any trouble in here."

"The trouble has already been done, Barkeep." Another man replied. "They're foreigners. They should be run out a town on a rail, so, since we have no rail, we'll just show them the door after a little American beat down for bein' here where they're not wanted."

Kevin made the sound of spitting in one hand, then rubbed both hands together.

He then said, "That's it, Lad. I've had enough of these uncouth, belligerent, illiterate, backwoods, obnoxious, self-assertive slobs. If it's a fight they want, then it's a fight they'll get."

Tim sighed heavily, then said, "Now you've done it, Mates. You got him riled. We came in for a peaceful pint of ale, but you have made that impossible. Remember, you wanted this."

As the five rowdy men began to close the gap between them, and the three men at the bar, in walked the sheriff with his revolver drawn, and at the ready. The sheriff, then came pushing through the swinging doors.

As they flapped back and forth, the sheriff said, "Alright. What's goin' on here?"

He came to stand between the five rowdy men, and the three men at the bar.

The bartender then said, "These three men came in, and from their manner of speech, I'd say they came from Scotland, and these five men took offense to that, and began to harass them."

Tim rebutted with, "That would be Ireland, Mate. We're Irishmen, but it does seem bein' Irish is against the law. Is that right, Sheriff?"

"The name's, Sheriff Prescott. Grant Prescott, and no, bein' Irish is not against the law."

Tim then said, "Then, you might want to let these blokes know it isn't against the law to be Irish. They seem to be vague in that area."

Sheriff Prescott then asked, "Were these five men harassin' these Irishmen, Clem?"

Clem answered, "Yes, that's the way it went down, Sheriff."

Sheriff Prescott turned to the five rowdy men saying, "You have five minutes to get out a town, or I'll toss all five a you in jail."

Reese wailed, "Jail!? On what charge!?"

"Threat of bodily harm, and disturbin' the peace." Sheriff Prescott replied.

Reese wailed again, "Disturbin' the peace!? In a saloon!?"

Sheriff Prescott said, "I can always up the charges to aggravated assault with a ten dollar fine, and a day in jail. Make up your mind."

Homer wailed this time with, "We never touched them! You can't prove we had an intent of aggravated assault."

Sheriff Prescott, then said, "Then, I'll toss your butts in jail for your own protection."

Another rowdy man wailed, "Our own protec..!? From who!?"

Sheriff Prescott answered as he pointed to Tim, Kevin, and Clancy saying, "Them."

The same man then said, "You've got to be kiddin' me! Them!?"

Sheriff Prescott replied, "I take it you have never heard the term, 'the fightin' Irish', have you?"

"What has that got to do with this?" The man asked. "The fightin' Irish." He scoffed, then said, "What does that mean?"

Sheriff Prescott answered, "It means that the Irish has made a science out of fighting. No matter how you think you have handled them, they have the science to knock you off your handle. So, I wouldn't want to be the one to get them angry. That would be one great big mistake."

Reese replied, "Aw, Sheriff, you're just tryin' to scare us, ain't you?"

Sheriff Prescott answered, "Yes, I am. You'll not win this struggle should you elect to try. So, here's the deal. I'd be getting out a town rather quickly were I you, or I'll let these three Irishmen have at you."

Reese turned to Tim, Kevin, and Clancy saying, "We'll leave, but this is far from over. We'll meet again somewhere, sometime, and when we do, you will rue the day this ever came 'bout."

Tim then said, "You brought this on yourself, Mister. All of you did. We tried to avoid trouble, but, you just had to keep pushin' it. So, live with the outcome of your decision."

Reese then said, "No one makes a fool out a Reese Burdette. No one, and gets away with it. Not for long they don't."

Clancy replied, "You have only yourself to blame for that."

Sheriff Prescott nudged, "Get along now. Go on. Get out a here, and get out a town, or I'll lock you all up, and let these fellas in your cells, and lock your cell doors."

Reese chuckled then said, "It almost seems worth it, doesn't it, fellas?"

Another man spoke saying, "Let's just move on, Reese. We've had our fun."

Reese replied, "You don't believe that hogwash the sheriff said do ya, Elmer?"

Elmer said, "I don't know what to believe any more, Reese. I do believe in the sayin', 'The fightin' Irish'. I've heard it said often enough that I believe it. I'd like to just mosey on down the road, and leave Cameron, Texas to those who live here. It won't break my heart to mount up, and git."

Reese turned to his remaining two friends, Quin Lawson, and Douglas Evers asking, "What 'bout you two?"

Before they could answer, Sheriff Prescott said, "I believe I told you fellas to move on and get on out a town. Now, move!"

Reese answered saying, "We're leavin', Sheriff. No need to push. I don't like it when I'm bein' pushed."

Sheriff Prescott then said, "Then, I suggest you move, and move now so I don't have to push you, but, push you I will."

As the five men moved to the swinging doors, they side stepped aside tables and chairs to get there. When they did get there, Reese pushed one side of the doors open, then stopped, and stared back.

Reese then said, "I'll be seein' you fellas. Real soon."

Then, Reese let the door go and then both doors began to flap back and forth, and then stopped.

Clancy shook his head in disbelief, then said, "Not only do we have the Caddo Indians to worry 'bout, we also have the Karankawa Indians to worry 'bout, and now, these jokers."

Tim turned to Clem, the bartender asking, "Did they say where they was goin' when they leave here?"

Clem answered, "No, Sir. They never said where they came from, nor where they were goin', 'course, I never asked either. You stay healthy that way."

Sheriff Prescott then said, "You fellas be careful when you leave. You just never know when, and if they will come back for retribution. It's best if you stay the night."

Kevin replied, "Already registered at the hotel for the night, Sheriff."

"Good." The sheriff said. "Well, I expect I should be doin' my rounds, so, you fellas have a good eve'nin'."

Tim said, "You as well, Sheriff. Be careful. There are all manner of man walking the streets at night."

Sheriff Prescott then said, "I am well aware of that fact, thanks. Well, good night."

Captain Rolo Quimby sat his horse listening to Corporal Wirt Jensen give his report as his troop streamed yards behind him.

When the report was given, Captain Quimby said, "Good report, Corporal. It'll show on your service record."

Corporal Jensen replied, "Thank you, Captain."

Captain Quimby then said, "Let's not doddle. Lieutenant Temple?"

1st Lieutenant, Boyd Temple answered, "Sir?"

Captain Quimby then said, "You have the troop, Lieutenant."

1st Lieutenant Temple replied, "Very well, Sir. Troop at a canter, forward ho!"

The troop moved out in staggered stages along the line at near canter.

Captain Quimby called from the front of the troop, "Private Streat? Front and center, Mister."

With the troop movement, Private Streat left the troop, and reined in beside Captain Quimby.

Private Streat said, "Yes, Sir, Captain."

Captain Quimby, then said, "You're at liberty, Private, to rejoin your column."

Streat replied, "Thank you, Sir."

"When you get there," Captain Quimby said. "Let them be aware that we will be there within the next quarter hour."

Private Streat said, "Thank you, Sir. I'll do that, Captain."

Captain Quimby then said, "Lieutenant Temple? I have the troop, Sir."

Private Streat left the troop, and rode hard for the column of Captain Locke and Captain Udall. And, true to his word, Captain Quimby, and the troop came in sight of the column in a little over 12 minutes, give, or take a minute. Captains Locke, and Udall left the column at a canter, and met Captain Quimby half way, leaving 1st Lieutenant Micah Chapman in charge of the column. He was joined by 1st Lieutenant Cole Trenton under Captain Silas Udall. Captain Rolo Quimby called a halt to the troop as both captains rode out to meet them.

Captain Locke, then said. "I'm mighty glad to see you, Captain. You, and B, troop."

Captain Quimby replied, "And, I you, Sir."

Captain Locke said, "Captain Quimby, this is Captain Udall out of Fort Arbuckle."

Captain Quimby then said, "I heard of your run in with the Comanche, Captain. I am sorry for the loss of your men, Sir."

Captain Udall gave a look of disappointment and sadness, then said, "As I am,

Sir. We were completely outnumbered. They laid a trap that was second to none, Captain, and I ran right into it."

Captain Quimby then said, "You had no way of knowing, Captain, so, don't beat yourself up for something you had no control over. You were simply outnumbered, and I am quite certain you did the best you could under those circumstances."

Captain Udall replied, "Thank you, Captain for those kind words."

Captain Quimby then said, "Well, Captains, shall we get these troopers home?"

Captain Locke then suggested, "I suggest we have joint command, which only seems feasible. Do you agree?"

Captain Quimby, and Captain Udall agreed to that arrangement, until a question came up.

Captain Udall then asked, "If we are attacked by Indians, who takes command of the column in that situation, or do we command our own troops?"

Captain Locke replied, "We'll discuss that as we go along, but I believe the highest ranking officer with years of service in that rank take command, whoever that may be."

Captain Udall turned to Captain Quimby asking, "Is that satisfactory to you, Sir?'

Captain Quimby replied, "I agree to that stipulation, Sir."

Captain Locke then said, "Very well. Then, let's get these people home." Captain Locke turned to the column of wagons and hollered, "Let's move out!"

All up and down the line troopers on those wagons were shouting at their draft horses to giddy-up, and shouts of, 'Yo', shattered the stillness, as they slapped the reins over their horses' backs. The wagons creaked and groaned under their heavy load. A few of the mounted troopers laid back to form a mounted skirmish line in protection by the rear guard. A defensive movement orchestrated by 1st Lieutenant Micah Chapman. Just then, scout Ned Grayson came riding back to the column in a hurry. When he reined in beside Captain Locke, the column kept moving. Ned finally reported that a wagon train a few miles from where they were was under attack by the Apache. The wagons were in a defensive circle, but they were heavily outnumbered.

They were in a great need of being rescued. All three Captains agreed to the rescue mission. Captain Udall asked to be in command of that rescue mission. Captain Locke and Captain Quimby agreed to it. Captain Udall then gathered his troopers, and Captain Quimby added a few more troopers for a better offence against the Apache. Then, the rescue mission took off from the column, with Ned Grayson leading the way to the struggling, and beleaguered wagon train. As they got closer to the battle that raged, the gunfire was heavy and extremely loud. Bodies of both Indian, and white man lay everywhere. Captain Udall then ordered that the troopers spread out left to right, then he led the charge and went riding into the midst of the Apache, and the wagon train. More Indians began to fall from their ponies due to the onslaught of the troopers and their weaponry. The troopers soon had the Apache on the run as they attempted to flee from the guns of the cavalry troop.

When the battle had ended, the Apache went racing away, yelling their warbling war cry as they left the field of battle.

Captain Udall hollered, "Bugler, sound recall."

Then, the bugler sounded recall, and the troopers who were in hot pursuit of the fleeing Apache gave up the chase, and reformed themselves.

Captain Udall then hollered, "Lieutenant Trenton, casualty report as soon as possible, Sir."

Lieutenant Trenton replied, "Yes, Sir." He turned in his saddle saying, "1st Sergeant, casualty report, ASAP."

1st Sergeant Jeremiah Sanaday replied, "Yes, Sir. Right away, Sir."

Chapter Ten

It ain't natural

Captain Udall searched out the wagon master of the wagon train, but he found out that the man was dead from an Apache arrow. There were a few dead men, a couple dead women, and what the most gruesome thing about this Apache attack was, there were dead children, two girls under the age of ten, and one boy just at ten years of age. Members of the wagon train walked around as if in a daze knowing it wouldn't take much for them to go over the edge of hysterics. Most had empty eyes due to this attack, and their countenance was sullen, dark, and demure to the point of being morose. Parents of the children who were killed wept openly as they were comforted by others in the wagon train. Everyone's nerves were set on edge, fragile, and tightly wound. The men of the wagon train thanked Captain Udall, and the troopers for their intervention that turned away. The beastly savages called, Apache. Upon returning to the column, Captain Udall and his troop of rescue gained an immediate prominence of respect for their rescue effort of the wagon train against the Apache. Casualty report reported two dead troopers, three wounded. Each had minor wounds. Captain Udall was commended for this action against the Apache by Captain Locke and Captain Quimby. They reaffirmed his rank and judgement in a hostile situation, creating in Captain Udall a debt of gratitude, and a sense of self-pride. He could again lift his head proudly while regaining his dignity in the eyes of the men in his command after the melee they was forced to endure, him and his men, at the rocky outcrop. He looked through new eyes, and he appreciated the newness of life. He sat straight in the saddle, tall, and proud. He was sure of himself thanks to the support of Captain Locke and Captain Quimby of Fort Richardson. No further indignation shall befall him.

Matt said of Slim, "That man is as sure footed as a mountain goat, and long on his convictions. It ain't often he is at a loss of what to do, or how to do it." He sighed, then said, "He seems lost just now. It's like he has lost his direction. It's sad to see this kind of behavior in a strong man such as Slim is. It ain't natural."